GREAT EXPECTATIONS

THE GRAPHIC NOVEL
Charles Dickens

QUICK TEXT VERSION

Script Adaptation: Jen Green
Character Designs & Original Artwork: John Stokes
Colouring: Digikore Studios Ltd.
Colour Finishing: Jason Cardy
Lettering: Jim Campbell
Design & Layout: Jo Wheeler & Jenny Placentino

Editor in Chief: Clive Bryant

Great Expectations: The Graphic Novel
Quick Text Version

Charles Dickens

First UK Edition

Published by: Classical Comics Ltd
Copyright ©2009 Classical Comics Ltd.

Acknowledgments: Every effort has been made to trace copyright holders of
material reproduced in this book. Any rights not acknowledged here will be
acknowledged in subsequent editions if notice is given to Classical Comics Ltd.

ISBN: 978-1-906332-11-2

Printed in the UK

This book is printed by 3P Direct Ltd. using biodegradable vegetable inks, on environmentally
friendly paper which is FSC (Forest Stewardship Council) certified (TT-COC-002291). This material
can be disposed of by recycling, incineration for energy recovery, composting and biodegradation.

The rights of Jen Green, John Stokes, Digikore Studios Ltd., Jason Cardy and Jim Campbell
to be identified as the artists of this work have been asserted in accordance with
the Copyright, Designs and Patents Act 1988 sections 77 and 78.

Contents

Dramatis Personæ

Young Pip
An orphan who lives with his sister and her husband

Adult Pip

Miss Havisham
An eccentric rich lady

Abel Magwitch
An escaped convict

Older Magwitch

Joe Gargery
Pip's brother-in-law

Mrs. Joe Gargery
Wife of Joe Gargery, and Pip's sister

Young Estella
Adopted daughter of Miss Havisham

Adult Estella

Young Biddy
Granddaughter to Mr. Wopsle's great aunt

Adult Biddy

Herbert Pocket
Son of Miss Havisham's cousin

Mr. Matthew Pocket
*Herbert's father
and Miss Havisham's cousin*

Sarah Pocket
Miss Havisham's cousin

Clara Barley
Fiancée to Herbert Pocket

Bentley Drummle
Student, taught by Matthew Pocket

Startop
Student, taught by Matthew Pocket

Mr. Jaggers
A lawyer from London

John Wemmick
Clerk to Mr. Jaggers

Aged Parent
Wemmick's father

Molly
Jaggers's housekeeper

Dolge Orlick
Works for Joe Gargery

Compeyson
A criminal

Mr. Pumblechook
Joe Gargery's uncle

Prologue

The year is 1812.

In the south-east corner of England, about thirty miles from the City of London, lies an area of marshland that separates the estuaries of the River Thames and the River Medway.

It's a cold, damp and misty area, home only to wildlife. There are a small number of villages nearby where a few countryside dwellings can be found, along with merchant traders, blacksmith's forges and public houses. There's also an old church that marks the end of life — before the desolate rough lands reach out towards the sea.

Far out from the shore lie floating prisons — converted warships called 'hulks' — that remove criminals from the overcrowded jails and keep them well away from society, while they await transportation to Australia and Tasmania. Murderers are hanged; but these ship-bound convicts are still considered dangerous enough to be banished from Britain for life.

This marshland is truly a bleak and barren place — the sort of place where someone could go unnoticed for a very long time; and where someone could stay hidden for as long as they wanted to hide…

I POINTED TOWARDS OUR **VILLAGE**, JUST OVER A MILE AWAY.

AAAAAAAAAAAAAAAAAAAAH!

YOU YOUNG **DOG**!

WHERE'S YOUR **MOTHER**?

THERE, SIR!

THERE'S MY MOTHER.

PIRRIP
...TE OF THIS PARISH
GEORGIANA
WIFE OF THE ABOVE

OH! AND IS THAT YOUR **FATHER** TOO?

YES, SIR.

HA! WHO D'YOU **LIVE** WITH THEN? SUPPOSIN' I **LET** YOU LIVE.

MY **SISTER**, MRS. GARGERY – WIFE OF JOE GARGERY, THE **BLACKSMITH**, SIR.

BLACKSMITH, EH? NOW LOOKEE HERE – YOU KNOW WHAT A **FILE** IS? YOU GET ME A FILE AND SOME **FOOD**.

YOU BRING 'EM TO ME HERE EARLY TOMORROW MORNING --

-- OR I'LL HAVE YOUR **HEART** AND **LIVER** OUT!

NOW, WHAT DO YOU **SAY?**

I **WILL** GET YOU THE FILE AND SOME FOOD.

I AIN'T **ALONE** HERE.

THERE'S A YOUNG MAN HIDING WITH ME, WHO'LL **KILL** YOU AS QUICK AS **LOOK** AT YOU.

I SAW HIM GO AND TURNED AWAY.

I LOOKED ALL ROUND FOR THE **OTHER** MAN; BUT I COULDN'T SEE HIM. **FRIGHTENED**, I RAN HOME.

WHERE IS THE **FIRING** FROM, MRS. JOE?

OH, THIS **BOY!** FROM THE **HULKS!**

WHAT ARE HULKS?

ANSWER HIM **ONE** QUESTION, AND HE'LL ASK YOU A **DOZEN** MORE! HULKS ARE **PRISON-SHIPS**, RIGHT ACROSS THE MARSHES.

WHY ARE THEY THERE?

I DIDN'T BRING YOU UP BY HAND TO **ANNOY** ME! PEOPLE ARE PUT THERE BECAUSE THEY DO ALL SORTS OF **BAD** THINGS – AND THEY ALWAYS **BEGIN** BY ASKING **QUESTIONS!** NOW, GET TO BED!

IT WAS **CHRISTMAS EVE.** IF I SLEPT AT **ALL** THAT NIGHT, IT WAS ONLY TO IMAGINE **MYSELF** ON ONE OF THE HULKS.

AS SOON AS IT STARTED TO GET LIGHT, I WENT **DOWNSTAIRS.**

I STOLE **FOOD** AND SOME **BRANDY** FROM A STONE BOTTLE – WHICH I TOPPED UP WITH WATER...

...AND I STOLE A BEAUTIFUL **PORK PIE.**

THEN I TOOK A **FILE** FROM JOE'S WORKSHOP...

...AND **RAN** TO THE **MARSHES.**

VOLUME I
CHAPTER III

I CROSSED A DITCH NEAR THE BATTERY, AND SAW A **MAN** SITTING BEFORE ME.

I WENT FORWARD **SOFTLY** AND TOUCHED HIM ON THE **SHOULDER**.

IT WAS **NOT** THE SAME MAN!

IT MUST BE THE **OTHER** MAN.

HE **STUMBLED** AND **RAN OFF**.

SOON I FOUND THE **RIGHT** MAN WAITING FOR ME.

I **GAVE** HIM WHAT I HAD **TAKEN**.

I'M SORRY, I CAN'T GET ANY **MORE** FOR YOUR **FRIEND**.

WHO?

THE **OTHER** MAN THAT YOU SPOKE OF.

HE DOESN'T **NEED** ANY.

HE **LOOKED** AS IF HE DID. JUST NOW, OVER THERE.

SHOW ME THE WAY HE WENT -- I'LL **GET** 'IM!

CURSE THIS IRON ON MY SORE LEG! GIVE US THE **FILE**, BOY.

HE WAS SOON FILING HIS IRON LIKE A **MADMAN**.

I WAS **SCARED** – AND SO I RAN AWAY.

VOLUME I
CHAPTER IV

I FULLY EXPECTED TO FIND A **POLICEMAN** WAITING FOR ME IN THE KITCHEN – BUT NO ONE HAD NOTICED THE **ROBBERY** YET.

MRS. JOE WAS **BUSY** GETTING THE HOUSE READY FOR CHRISTMAS DINNER.

AND **WHERE** HAVE YOU BEEN?

TO HEAR THE **CAROLS**.

PERHAPS IF I WARN'T A **SLAVE** HERE, I SHOULD HAVE GONE TO HEAR THE CAROLS, **TOO**.

JOE CROSSED HIS FINGERS TO SHOW ME THAT SHE WAS IN A CROSS TEMPER.

MR. WOPSLE ARRIVED, AS WELL AS MR. AND MRS. HUBBLE, AND JOE'S UNCLE PUMBLECHOOK – A WELL-TO-DO CORN MERCHANT.

I HAVE BROUGHT YOU A BOTTLE OF **SHERRY** AND A BOTTLE OF **PORT**.

OH, UN--CLE PUM-BLE--CHOOK! HOW **KIND**!

THEY WOULDN'T LEAVE ME **ALONE**. IT BEGAN WHEN MR. WOPSLE SAID GRACE.

...MAY WE BE TRULY GRATEFUL.

DO YOU **HEAR** THAT? BE **GRATEFUL**!

BE **GRATEFUL**, BOY, TO **THEM** WHICH BROUGHT YOU UP BY **HAND**.

HAVE SOME BRANDY, UNCLE.

O NO! IT'S **WEAK**!

TAR!

I HAD FILLED UP THE BOTTLE WITH **TAR-WATER** BY **MISTAKE**!

HOW DID **TAR** GET IN THERE?

UNCLE PUMBLECHOOK **WAVED** IT AWAY – I THOUGHT I HAD GOT AWAY WITH IT, UNTIL MY SISTER SAID...

TO FINISH WITH, YOU **MUST** TASTE OUR DELIGHTFUL **PORK PIE**.

GOODNESS ME! WHERE'S IT **GONE?**

I RAN FOR MY LIFE.

HERE YOU ARE, LOOK **SHARP!**

VOLUME I
CHAPTER V

EXCUSE ME, LADIES AND GENTLEMEN, BUT I AM ON A **CHASE** IN THE NAME OF THE KING, AND WANT THE **BLACKSMITH!**

WHAT **FOR?**

THESE **HANDCUFFS** ARE FAULTY, AND WE NEED THEM REPAIRED.

THEY WERE NOT FOR **ME**, AND THE PIE HAD BEEN **FORGOTTEN**. JOE WENT TO THE FORGE.

WHEN FINISHED, HE SUGGESTED WE GO ALONG WITH THE SOLDIERS. WE WERE TOLD TO STAY **BACK** AND KEEP **QUIET.**

I hope we **don't** find them.

I bet we **do.**

I **DREADED** THAT THE CONVICT WOULD THINK I HAD BROUGHT THE SOLDIERS THERE.

WE HEARD **SHOUTING** FROM A DISTANCE.

AT THE DOUBLE!

MURDER!

CONVICTS! THIS WAY!

HERE THEY ARE!

SURRENDER, YOU TWO!

REMEMBER I **TOOK** HIM! I **GAVE** HIM TO YOU!

IT WON'T DO YOU ANY **GOOD.**

GUARD – HE TRIED TO **MURDER** ME!

HE'S A LIAR!

ENOUGH!

LIGHT THOSE TORCHES!

MARCH!

WHEN MY CONVICT SAW ME, HE GAVE ME A LOOK THAT I DIDN'T **UNDERSTAND.**

AFTER AN HOUR OF TRAVELLING, WE GOT TO THE LANDING-PLACE.

I MUST SAY SOMETHING --

-- I TOOK SOME FOOD AND DRINK FROM THE BLACKSMITH'S IN THE VILLAGE.

MY WIFE SAW THEY WERE MISSING.

SO YOU'RE THE BLACKSMITH, ARE YOU? I'M SORRY – I'VE EATEN YOUR PIE.

YOU'RE WELCOME TO IT. WHATEVER YOU'VE DONE, WE WOULDN'T HAVE YOU STARVED TO DEATH FOR IT, WOULD WE, PIP?

VOLUME I
CHAPTER VI

THEY TOOK THE CONVICTS BACK TO THE HULKS BY TORCHLIGHT.

I HAD GOT AWAY WITH IT, BUT I KEPT THE TRUTH SECRET.

MR. WOPSLE'S GREAT-AUNT KEPT AN EVENING SCHOOL IN THE VILLAGE. THE CHILDREN PAID HER TWO PENCE A WEEK TO BE THERE, BUT SHE SPENT MOST OF THE TIME **SLEEPING**.

WITH THE HELP OF HER GRANDDAUGHTER **BIDDY**, I STRUGGLED THROUGH THE ALPHABET. LIKE ME, BIDDY WAS AN **ORPHAN** WHO HAD BEEN BROUGHT UP BY HAND.

ONE NIGHT I MANAGED TO **WRITE** A **LETTER** TO JOE.

Mi deer Jo i ope u r kr wite well i ope i shal son b habell 4 2 teedge u jo an then we shorl b so gladd an wen i m prengtd 2 u jo wot larx an bleve me inf xn PiP

I SAY, PIP, OLD CHAP! YOU'RE A **SCHOLAR**.

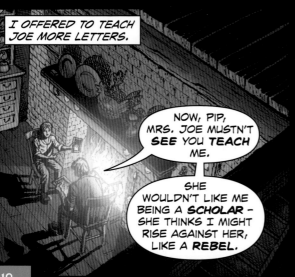

I OFFERED TO TEACH JOE MORE LETTERS.

NOW, PIP, MRS. JOE MUSTN'T **SEE** YOU **TEACH** ME.

SHE WOULDN'T LIKE ME BEING A **SCHOLAR** – SHE THINKS I MIGHT RISE AGAINST HER, LIKE A **REBEL**.

YOUR SISTER'S **HARD** ON US, BUT I DON'T RISE – 'CAUSE SHE'S **SMART** AND I'M **NOT**.

IT'S NEARLY EIGHT O'CLOCK – SHE'LL BE **BACK** SOON.

HERE SHE COMES **NOW**.

THIS BOY HAD BETTER BE **GRATEFUL** FOR WHAT WE'VE DONE FOR HIM TONIGHT. SHE'D BETTER NOT **PAMPER** HIM.

SHE **WON'T**.

SHE?

MISS **HAVISHAM** — SHE WANTS PIP TO GO AND **PLAY** THERE — AND HE'D **BETTER** GO THERE, TOO.

MISS HAVISHAM WAS A VERY **RICH** AND **MISERABLE** LADY WHO LIVED LOCKED AWAY IN A **LARGE** AND **DISMAL** HOUSE.

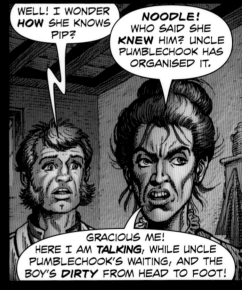

WELL! I WONDER **HOW** SHE KNOWS PIP?

NOODLE! WHO SAID SHE **KNEW** HIM? UNCLE PUMBLECHOOK HAS ORGANISED IT.

GRACIOUS ME! HERE I AM **TALKING**, WHILE UNCLE PUMBLECHOOK'S WAITING, AND THE BOY'S **DIRTY** FROM HEAD TO FOOT!

SPLOOSH

BOY, BE FOREVER **GRATEFUL** TO ALL FRIENDS, BUT ESPECIALLY UNTO THEM WHICH BROUGHT YOU UP BY HAND!

I WAS THEN HANDED OVER TO MR. PUMBLECHOOK.

GOD BLESS YOU, PIP!

VOLUME I
CHAPTER VIII

NEXT MORNING, WE WENT TO SATIS HOUSE – THE **HOME** OF MISS HAVISHAM.

THIS IS PIP.

THIS IS **PIP**, IS IT? COME **IN**, PIP.

QUICKLY, BOY!

WE WENT INTO THE HOUSE BY A SIDE DOOR. **ALL** INSIDE WAS **DARK.**

FINALLY, WE CAME TO A DOOR.

AFTER YOU, MISS.

DON'T BE **SILLY** – **I'M** NOT GOING IN.

SHE WALKED AWAY, AND TOOK THE CANDLE WITH HER.

KNOCK

KNOCK

ENTER!

YOU SAY **NOTHING** OF HER, EVEN THOUGH SHE IS HARSH TOWARDS YOU. WHAT DO YOU **THINK** OF HER?

I think she is very **pretty**... ...and **very insulting.**

ANYTHING ELSE?

I'd like to go **home.**

YOU SHALL GO **SOON.** FINISH THE GAME FIRST.

WE FINISHED, AND ESTELLA THREW THE CARDS DOWN ON THE TABLE AS IF SHE **HATED** THEM.

LET ME THINK WHEN I SHALL HAVE YOU HERE **AGAIN**...

COME AGAIN AFTER **SIX DAYS.**

ESTELLA, LET HIM HAVE SOMETHING TO **EAT** BEFORE HE **GOES.**

I WAS TAKEN BACK OUTSIDE.

YOU ARE TO WAIT HERE, BOY.

SHE DISAPPEARED AND CLOSED THE DOOR.

ALONE IN THE COURTYARD, I LOOKED AT MY COARSE HANDS AND MY COMMON BOOTS. THEY HAD NEVER TROUBLED ME **BEFORE**, BUT I **DISLIKED** THEM NOW.

SHE CAME BACK AND GAVE ME FOOD AND DRINK, AS IF I WERE A **DOG** IN **DISGRACE.**

I WAS SO **HURT** THAT I HAD TO HOLD BACK MY TEARS.

BUT WHEN SHE HAD **GONE,** I HID MY FACE AND CRIED.

LOOKING AROUND ME, I ENTERED AN OVERGROWN GARDEN AND FOUND AN OLD BREWERY.

SUDDENLY, I SAW A FIGURE **HANGING** FROM A BEAM...

...IT WAS **MISS HAVISHAM!**

I WAS EVEN **MORE** FRIGHTENED WHEN I REALISED THERE WAS NO ONE THERE.

GASP!

THE LIGHT CALMED ME, AND I SAW **ESTELLA** APPROACHING WITH THE KEYS TO LET ME OUT.

WHY DON'T YOU **CRY**?

BECAUSE I DON'T **WANT** TO.

YOU **DO**. YOU HAVE BEEN CRYING **ALREADY**, AND YOU ARE CLOSE TO CRYING **AGAIN** NOW.

HA, HA, HA!

SHE **LOCKED** THE GATE BEHIND ME. I SET OFF ON THE **LONG** WALK HOME, THINKING THAT MY **HANDS** WERE **COARSE**, MY **BOOTS** WERE **THICK**, AND THAT I WAS A **COMMON LABOURING BOY.**

25

WHEN I REACHED HOME, THEY WANTED TO KNOW ALL ABOUT MY DAY. I WAS SURE THAT THEY WOULDN'T BELIEVE WHAT HAD *ACTUALLY* HAPPENED.

VOLUME I
CHAPTER IX

WELL, BOY, HOW DID YOU GET ON?

PRETTY WELL, SIR.

PRETTY WELL IS NO ANSWER. *WHAT* WAS MISS HAVISHAM *DOING* WHEN YOU GOT THERE?

SHE WAS SITTING IN A BLACK VELVET *COACH*. AND MISS ESTELLA – THAT'S HER NIECE, I THINK – HANDED HER CAKE AND WINE ON A *GOLD* PLATE.

WE ALL HAD CAKE AND WINE ON GOLD PLATES.

IN A BLACK VELVET COACH? CAN THIS BE *POSSIBLE*, UNCLE?

I THINK HE *MEANS* A SEDAN-CHAIR.

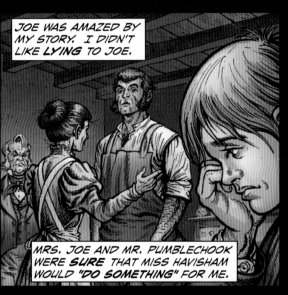

JOE WAS AMAZED BY MY STORY. I DIDN'T LIKE *LYING* TO JOE.

MRS. JOE AND MR. PUMBLECHOOK WERE *SURE* THAT MISS HAVISHAM WOULD "*DO SOMETHING*" FOR ME.

AFTER MR. PUMBLECHOOK HAD GONE, I WENT TO SEE JOE IN THE FORGE.

JOE, DO YOU REMEMBER WHAT I SAID ABOUT MISS HAVISHAM'S?

IT'S A *TERRIBLE* THING, BUT IT AIN'T *TRUE*.

PIP, OLD CHAP! THIS WON'T *DO*, OLD FELLOW! THAT'S *AWFUL*!

I TOLD JOE THAT I FELT *MISERABLE*, AND HOW I WISHED I WAS NOT COMMON, AND HAD *LIED* TO COVER IT UP.

LIES ARE LIES, AND THEY'RE *WRONG*. AND AS TO BEING COMMON, WELL YOU'RE UNCOMMON IN SOME THINGS – YOU'RE AN UNCOMMON *SCHOLAR*.

NO, I AM IGNORANT AND *BACKWARD*, JOE.

WELL, PIP, EVERYONE – EVEN A *KING* – STARTS BY BEING A *COMMON* SCHOLAR BEFORE THEY CAN BE AN *UNCOMMON* ONE.

I FOUND HOPE IN THIS PIECE OF WISDOM.

I DECIDED THAT THE BEST THING I COULD DO WAS TO ASK BIDDY FOR *HELP*. I TOLD HER THAT I WISHED TO GET ON IN LIFE, AND WANTED TO KNOW *EVERYTHING* THAT SHE KNEW.

VOLUME I
CHAPTER X

BIDDY *AGREED* TO HELP ME, AND WE BEGAN THAT NIGHT.

THERE WAS A PUBLIC-HOUSE IN THE VILLAGE, CALLED THE **THREE JOLLY BARGEMEN.** MY SISTER TOLD ME TO COLLECT JOE FROM THERE ON THE WAY HOME FROM SCHOOL.

I FOUND HIM THERE, SMOKING HIS PIPE WITH MR. WOPSLE AND A **STRANGER.**

THE STRANGER LOOKED **HARD** AT ME, NODDED, AND MADE ROOM FOR ME BESIDE HIM.

I SAT NEXT TO JOE INSTEAD.

YOU'RE THE **BLACKSMITH,** THEN, MR. GARGERY? WHAT'LL YOU DRINK?

VERY KIND – **RUM!**

THREE RUMS IT IS!

I DON'T KNOW 'ROUND HERE – DO **MANY** PEOPLE LIVE OVER ON THE MARSHES?

THE STRANGER LOOKED AT ME **AGAIN AND WINKED.**

NO. WE GET A RUNAWAY **CONVICT** NOW AND THEN. AND WE DON'T FIND THEM VERY OFTEN – EH, MR. WOPSLE?

YOU'VE BEEN OUT **LOOKING** FOR SOME?

JUST ONCE.

HE'S A LIKELY YOUNG LAD – WHAT'S HIS **NAME?**

PIP.

27

I SAW HIM STIR HIS RUM WITH A *FILE*.

NO ONE ELSE SAW IT.

I KNEW IT WAS THE ONE I'D *TAKEN*, SO HE MUST HAVE KNOWN MY CONVICT.

AFTER HIS DRINK, JOE GOT UP TO LEAVE.

STOP A MOMENT, MR. GARGERY — I THINK I'VE GOT A BRIGHT NEW *SHILLING* IN MY POCKET FOR THE BOY.

YOURS! MIND — YOUR OWN.

THANK YOU.

HE FOLDED IT IN SOME CRUMPLED PAPER.

MY SISTER WAS IN A GOOD MOOD WHEN WE GOT HOME, SO JOE TOLD HER ABOUT THE BRIGHT SHILLING.

LET'S LOOK AT IT.

BUT WHAT'S *THIS*?

TWO ONE-POUND NOTES?

JOE RAN BACK TO THE PUBLIC-HOUSE WITH THEM, BUT THE MAN HAD *GONE*. JOE LEFT A MESSAGE FOR HIM, AND MY SISTER *HID* THE MONEY IN A TEAPOT.

ON MY **NEXT** VISIT TO MISS HAVISHAM'S, ESTELLA LED ME TO A **DIFFERENT** PART OF THE HOUSE.

VOLUME I
CHAPTER XI

YOU ARE TO COME THIS WAY TODAY.

SHE LED ME TO A DETACHED DWELLING-HOUSE. WE ENTERED A **GLOOMY** ROOM WHERE THREE LADIES AND A GENTLEMAN WERE TALKING.

THEY **STOPPED** TO LOOK AT ME WHEN I ENTERED.

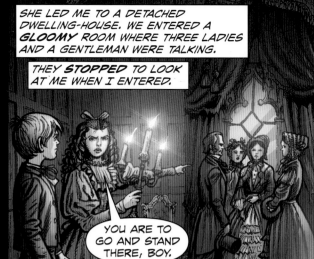

YOU ARE TO GO AND STAND THERE, BOY.

POOR **DEAR** SOUL! MATTHEW IS NOBODY'S ENEMY BUT HIS **OWN**!

WE ARE TO **LOVE** OUR NEIGHBOUR.

POOR SOUL! HE IS SO VERY **STRANGE**!

DING A LING

NOW, BOY!

AS WE WERE GOING ALONG THE DARK PASSAGE, ESTELLA SUDDENLY **STOPPED** AND **FACED** ME.

AM I **PRETTY**?

YES, YOU ARE.

AM I **INSULTING**?

NOT AS MUCH AS **LAST** TIME.

SMACK!

WHAT DO YOU THINK OF ME **NOW**, YOU COARSE LITTLE MONSTER?

I WON'T TELL YOU.

WHICH WAS A **LIE**, BECAUSE I WAS CRYING INSIDE.

WHY DON'T YOU **CRY**, YOU LITTLE WRETCH?

BECAUSE I'LL **NEVER** CRY FOR YOU **AGAIN**.

FURTHER ON, WE MET A GENTLEMAN.

WHOM HAVE WE HERE? BOY OF THE NEIGHBOURHOOD, HEY? HOW DO **YOU** COME **HERE**?

WELL! BEHAVE YOURSELF. YOU BOYS ARE A **BAD** SET OF FELLOWS. MIND YOU **BEHAVE** YOURSELF!

MISS HAVISHAM SENT FOR ME, SIR.

WITH THOSE WORDS, HE RELEASED ME AND WENT ON HIS WAY.

WE WERE SOON IN MISS HAVISHAM'S ROOM. ESTELLA LEFT ME STANDING NEAR THE DOOR.

ARE YOU READY TO **PLAY**?

I DON'T THINK I **AM**, MA'AM.

THEN ARE YOU WILLING TO **WORK**?

YES.

THEN GO INTO THE ROOM OPPOSITE, AND **WAIT** FOR ME.

I CROSSED THE LANDING AND ENTERED THE DARK ROOM. EVERYTHING WAS COVERED IN **DUST** AND **MOULD**, AND WAS **FALLING APART**.

A FEAST HAD BEEN PREPARED, BUT IT SEEMED LIKE **EVERYTHING** IN THE HOUSE, INCLUDING THE **CLOCKS**, HAD **FROZEN** IN TIME.

THAT'S **MY** WEDDING CAKE OVER THERE.

COME, COME! WALK ME!

I HAD TO WALK MISS HAVISHAM AROUND THE ROOM.

DEAR MISS HAVISHAM! HOW **WELL** YOU LOOK!

I DO **NOT**, SARAH POCKET! I AM YELLOW SKIN AND BONE.

MISS HAVISHAM **WASN'T** FOOLED BY HER **WORDS.**

MATTHEW **NEVER** COMES HERE TO SEE YOU.

HE WILL COME AND SEE ME, WHEN I AM LAID OUT ON THAT TABLE.

THAT WILL BE HIS PLACE – THERE – AT MY HEAD!

YOU ALL KNOW WHERE TO SIT WHEN I **DIE.**

NOW GO!

I SUPPOSE WE **SHOULD**...

BLESS YOU, MISS HAVISHAM DEAR!

TODAY IS MY **BIRTHDAY**, PIP --

-- BUT I DON'T LIKE **THOSE** PEOPLE TO **TALK** ABOUT IT. IT WAS ON **THIS** DAY, LONG BEFORE YOU WERE BORN, THAT **ALL THIS** WAS BROUGHT HERE.

WE HAVE **WORN AWAY** TOGETHER.

SHE STOOD LOOKING AT THE TABLE, AND I KEPT QUIET.

ESTELLA RETURNED, AND A DAY WAS SET FOR MY **NEXT** VISIT. THEN I WAS TAKEN DOWN INTO THE YARD TO BE FED IN THE SAME **DOG-LIKE** MANNER.

AFTER A SHORT WALK AROUND THE GARDEN, I FOUND MYSELF BACK AT THE HOUSE. I LOOKED IN AT A WINDOW...

...AND SAW A PALE YOUNG GENTLEMAN.

HELLO, YOUNG FELLOW! WHO LET **YOU** IN?

MISS ESTELLA.

COME AND FIGHT!

WHAT ELSE COULD I **DO**?

AARRGH!

DOOFFF!

THWUMMPP!

AT LAST, HE FELL BADLY AND HIT HIS **HEAD**. HE THREW HIS SPONGE UP IN THE AIR.

≷GASP≷ THAT MEANS ≷GASP≷ YOU HAVE **WON**.

CAN I HELP YOU?

NO THANK YOU. ≷GASP≷ GOOD AFTERNOON.

ESTELLA WAS WAITING FOR ME IN THE COURTYARD, LOOKING **PLEASED**.

YOU MAY **KISS** ME, IF YOU LIKE.

I KISSED HER CHEEK...

...BUT I FELT THAT THE KISS WAS GIVEN TO THE COARSE COMMON BOY — LIKE **MONEY** IS GIVEN TO THE **POOR**.

VOLUME I
CHAPTER XII

BECAUSE OF THE FIGHT, I WAS **SCARED** TO LEAVE THE HOUSE. I WAS SURE THE OFFICERS OF THE COUNTY JAIL WOULD **ARREST** ME.

I WAS EVEN MORE AFRAID WHEN THE DAY CAME FOR ME TO **RETURN** TO MISS HAVISHAM'S...

...BUT THE PALE YOUNG GENTLEMAN WAS **NOWHERE** TO BE SEEN.

ONCE AGAIN, I HAD TO PUSH MISS HAVISHAM AROUND THE TWO ROOMS.

Does she grow **prettier** Pip?

Yes.

I PERFORMED THESE DUTIES EVERY OTHER DAY FOR NEARLY **TEN** MONTHS.

ESTELLA WAS ALWAYS THERE, BUT SHE DIDN'T LET ME KISS HER AGAIN. SOMETIMES SHE WOULD BE NICE TO ME, AND OTHER TIMES SHE'D BE HORRIBLE, TELLING ME THAT SHE **HATED** ME.

Break their **hearts** my pride and hope, break their hearts and have **no mercy!**

JOE CLOSED THE FORGE FOR THE DAY AND, IN HIS **BEST** CLOTHES, WENT WITH ME TO MISS HAVISHAM'S.

MY SISTER STAYED WITH UNCLE PUMBLECHOOK.

ESTELLA TOOK **NO** NOTICE OF **EITHER** OF US, BUT LED THE WAY THAT I KNEW SO **WELL**.

YOU ARE **BOTH** TO GO IN.

ALL THE TIME, JOE KEPT TALKING TO **ME** INSTEAD OF MISS HAVISHAM...

YOU HAVE RAISED PIP, AND INTEND TO MAKE HIM YOUR **APPRENTICE**, MR. GARGERY?

AS YOU AND ME ARE **FRIENDS**, I WOULDN'T HAVE **FORCED** YOU, PIP.

HAVE YOU BROUGHT HIS **PAPERS** WITH YOU?

WELL, PIP, YOU **SAW** ME BRING THEM.

YOU EXPECTED NO **MONEY** WITH THE BOY?

PIP, YOU **KNOW** THE ANSWER TO BE **NO**, PIP.

PIP HAS EARNED MONEY **HERE**. THERE ARE TWENTY-FIVE POUNDS IN THIS BAG. GIVE IT TO YOUR **MASTER**, PIP.

THIS IS **VERY** KIND OF YOU, PIP.

AND NOW, OLD CHAP, MAY YOU AND ME DO OUR **DUTY**!

GOODBYE, PIP! LET THEM OUT, ESTELLA.

AM I TO COME **AGAIN**, MISS HAVISHAM?

NO. **GARGERY** IS YOUR **MASTER** NOW.

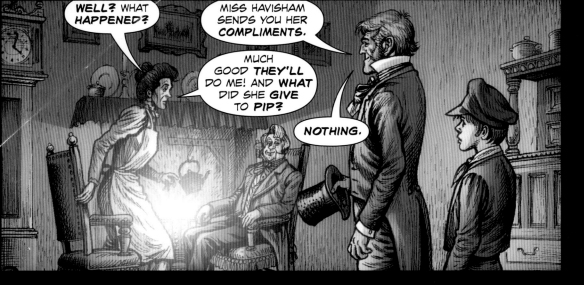

WELL? WHAT HAPPENED?

MISS HAVISHAM SENDS YOU HER COMPLIMENTS.

MUCH GOOD THEY'LL DO ME! AND WHAT DID SHE GIVE TO PIP?

NOTHING.

WHAT SHE GAVE, SHE GAVE TO YOU — TWENTY-FIVE POUNDS!

NOW YOU SEE HOW I AM SOMEONE WHO ALWAYS FINISHES WHAT I'VE BEGUN. THIS BOY MUST BE APPRENTICED RIGHT AWAY.

WE WENT TO THE COURT HOUSE TO HAVE ME BOUND AS JOE'S APPRENTICE.

TOWN HALL

What's he done?

He looks like a bad 'un.

MY SISTER DECIDED THAT WE SHOULD CELEBRATE WITH DINNER AT THE BLUE BOAR. IT WAS AWFUL.

PUMBLECHOOK TOOK THE TOP OF THE TABLE AND PUT ME ON A CHAIR BESIDE HIM.

THEY WOULDN'T LET ME GO TO SLEEP. THEY KEPT WAKING ME UP AND TELLING ME TO ENJOY MYSELF.

WHEN I FINALLY GOT TO BED, I FELT TERRIBLE. I DIDN'T THINK I'D EVER LIKE JOE'S TRADE.

I HAD LIKED IT ONCE, BUT NOT NOW.

IT'S AWFUL TO FEEL *ASHAMED* OF YOUR OWN HOME. MY *SISTER* HAD MADE MY HOME LIFE *UNPLEASANT* – BUT NOW IT ALSO SEEMED *COARSE* AND *COMMON.*

I *DREADED* THE THOUGHT OF BEING ALL GRIMY AND *COMMON* AT WORK, ONLY TO GLANCE UP AND SEE ESTELLA LOOKING IN AT THE FORGE, *DESPISING* ME.

VOLUME I CHAPTER XV

NOW THAT I WAS OLDER, MY *EDUCATION* CAME TO AN END. I TAUGHT JOE EVERYTHING I *KNEW...*

...NOT TO *HELP* HIM, BUT TO MAKE HIM *LESS* IGNORANT AND COMMON, SO THAT HE WOULD BE MORE *ACCEPTABLE* TO ESTELLA.

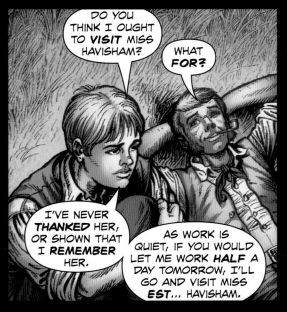

DO YOU THINK I OUGHT TO *VISIT* MISS HAVISHAM?

WHAT *FOR?*

I'VE NEVER *THANKED* HER, OR SHOWN THAT I *REMEMBER* HER.

AS WORK IS QUIET, IF YOU WOULD LET ME WORK *HALF* A DAY TOMORROW, I'LL GO AND VISIT MISS *EST...* HAVISHAM.

HER NAME *AIN'T ESTAVISHAM,* PIP!

I KNOW – *SORRY!* BUT WHAT DO YOU *THINK?*

JOE *AGREED,* BUT SAID THAT IF I WASN'T TREATED WELL THERE, I SHOULDN'T GO *AGAIN.*

JOE EMPLOYED AN UNPLEASANT WORKMAN CALLED ORLICK. HE **DISLIKED** ME AND BELIEVED I WOULD PUT HIM OUT OF A JOB.

NOW **MASTER**, IF YOUNG PIP HAS A HALF-HOLIDAY, SO SHOULD I.

WHY? WHAT'LL YOU **DO** WITH IT?

AS MUCH AS **HE** WILL.

NOW, MASTER! NO **FAVOURING** IN THIS SHOP. BE A **MAN**!

ALRIGHT THEN, LET IT BE A HALF-HOLIDAY FOR **ALL**.

YOU **FOOL**! GIVING HOLIDAYS TO GREAT IDLE **VILLAINS** LIKE THAT!

I WISH I WERE HIS **MASTER**!

IF YOU HAD **YOUR** WAY, YOU'D BE **EVERYBODY'S** MASTER.

LEAVE HER **ALONE**.

I'D BE A MATCH FOR ANY **ROGUE** LIKE **YOU**!

YOU'RE A **FOUL SHREW**, MOTHER GARGERY.

THWAAKK!

My sister **fainted**. Joe **carried** her into the house, and I **dressed** to go to Miss Havisham's.

Miss Sarah Pocket let me in. Everything was the same, except there was no **Estella**.

ARE YOU LOOKING ROUND FOR **ESTELLA?**

I H-H-HOPE THAT SHE IS W-W-WELL.

SHE IS ABROAD, LEARNING TO BE A **LADY.** DO YOU FEEL THAT YOU HAVE **LOST** HER? Heh-heh-heh...

I didn't know what to say, but she dismissed me before I could **answer**.

The visit made me dislike my **home** and my **work** more than **ever.**

I HAPPENED TO MEET WITH MR. WOPSLE AND, AFTER A VISIT TO UNCLE PUMBLECHOOK, WE WALKED HOME. ON THE WAY, WE STUMBLED ACROSS **ORLICK**.

THE **GUNS** ARE GOING AGAIN — SOME CONVICTS HAVE **ESCAPED** FROM THE HULKS.

WHEN WE REACHED THE JOLLY BARGEMEN, MR. WOPSLE WENT IN TO FIND OUT WHAT ALL THE **FUSS** WAS ABOUT.

PIP, YOUR **HOUSE** HAS BEEN BROKEN INTO.

SOMEONE'S BEEN **ATTACKED** AND **HURT**.

COME ON!

OUR KITCHEN WAS FULL OF **PEOPLE**, AND THE **DOCTOR** WAS **ALREADY** THERE.

MY SISTER WAS LYING **SENSELESS** ON THE FLOOR. SHE'D BEEN **HIT** ON THE BACK OF THE **HEAD**...

...AND THERE WAS A FILED **LEG-IRON** BY HER SIDE.

42

I BELIEVED IT WAS MY **CONVICT'S** LEG-IRON, BUT I DIDN'T THINK HE'D DONE THIS. I THOUGHT IT WAS EITHER **ORLICK**, OR THAT **STRANGER** WITH THE FILE.

THE **POLICE** FROM LONDON STAYED AROUND THE VILLAGE FOR A WEEK OR TWO, BUT THE VILLAIN WASN'T **FOUND**.

LONG AFTER THEY'D GONE, MY SISTER LAY **ILL** IN BED. HER SIGHT, HEARING, SPEECH AND MEMORY WERE ALL **AFFECTED**.

WHEN SHE FINALLY CAME DOWNSTAIRS, SHE COULDN'T **SPEAK** – SO SHE HAD TO WRITE THINGS DOWN ON MY SLATE.

EVEN SO, SHE WAS MUCH **CALMER**.

WHEN MR. WOPSLE'S GREAT-AUNT DIED, BIDDY **STAYED** WITH US TO HELP LOOK AFTER MY SISTER.

SHE QUICKLY BECAME A **BLESSING** TO US ALL, AND ESPECIALLY TO **JOE**.

43

I NOW FELL INTO A ROUTINE OF WORK, BROKEN **ONLY** BY BIRTHDAYS AND YEARLY VISITS TO SEE MISS HAVISHAM. I STARTED TO SEE A **CHANGE** IN BIDDY.

SHE WAS NOT **BEAUTIFUL** – SHE WAS COMMON AND WOULD NEVER BE LIKE **ESTELLA** – BUT SHE WAS **PLEASANT** AND **KIND**.

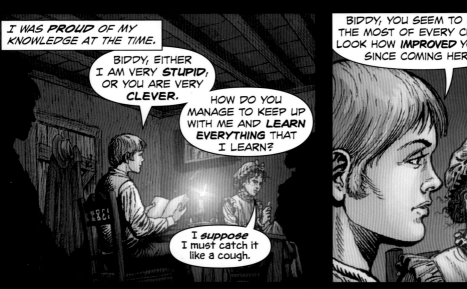

I WAS **PROUD** OF MY KNOWLEDGE AT THE TIME.

BIDDY, EITHER I AM VERY **STUPID**, OR YOU ARE VERY **CLEVER**.

HOW DO YOU MANAGE TO KEEP UP WITH ME AND **LEARN EVERYTHING** THAT I LEARN?

I *suppose* I must catch it like a cough.

BIDDY, YOU SEEM TO MAKE THE MOST OF EVERY CHANCE. LOOK HOW **IMPROVED** YOU ARE SINCE COMING HERE!

I WAS **YOUR** FIRST TEACHER, THOUGH.

YES, YOU **WERE**. AT THE TIME, I NEVER THOUGHT WE'D BE TOGETHER LIKE THIS.

LET'S GO FOR A **WALK** ON SUNDAY.

THAT SUNDAY, JOE LOOKED AFTER MY SISTER, WHILE BIDDY AND I WALKED TOGETHER. I THOUGHT IT WAS A GOOD TIME TO **CONFESS** SOMETHING TO HER.

BIDDY, I WANT TO BE A **GENTLEMAN**.

YOU KNOW **BEST**, PIP – BUT WOULDN'T YOU BE **HAPPIER** STAYING AS YOU **ARE**?

NO – I AM **DISGUSTED** WITH MY WORK AND MY **LIFE**.

I SHALL **NEVER** BE HAPPY AS I **AM**.

THAT'S A PITY!

IF I COULD HAVE SETTLED, MAYBE JOE AND I MIGHT HAVE RUN THE **FORGE** TOGETHER. I MIGHT EVEN HAVE SETTLED DOWN WITH **YOU**.

I'D HAVE BEEN GOOD **ENOUGH** FOR YOU, WOULDN'T I?

YES – I'M NOT **FUSSY**.

INSTEAD, I AM **UNHAPPY**.

BEING **COARSE** AND **COMMON** WOULDN'T MATTER IF **NOBODY** HAD **TOLD** ME THAT I WAS!

WHO SAID **THAT** TO YOU?

THE BEAUTIFUL YOUNG LADY AT MISS HAVISHAM'S. I ADMIRE HER **SO** MUCH; I WANT TO BE A GENTLEMAN FOR **HER**.

TO **SPITE** HER, OR TO WIN HER **HEART**?

I DIDN'T KNOW THE **ANSWER** TO THAT.

45

I HAD BEEN JOE'S APPRENTICE FOR FOUR YEARS WHEN, ONE SATURDAY NIGHT, A **STRANGER** CAME INTO THE JOLLY BARGEMAN.

I RECOGNISED HIM AS THE GENTLEMAN I HAD MET ON THE STAIRS ON MY SECOND VISIT TO MISS HAVISHAM.

I HAVE REASON TO BELIEVE THERE IS A **BLACKSMITH** HERE CALLED **JOE GARGERY.**

HERE I AM.

IS YOUR **APPRENTICE,** PIP, HERE?

I AM!

I NEED TO TALK TO YOU BOTH IN **PRIVATE.** SHALL WE GO TO YOUR **HOME?**

PUZZLED, WE WALKED HOME IN **SILENCE.**

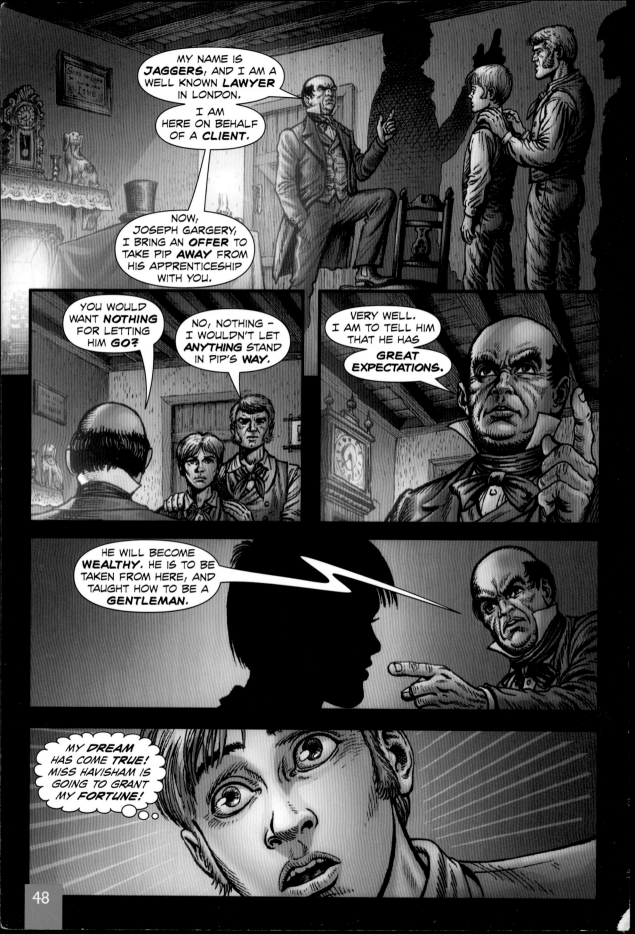

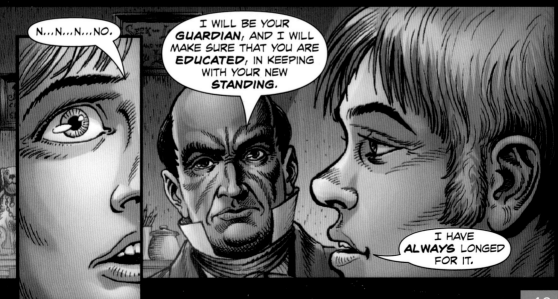

YOU SHALL BE TAUGHT BY MR. **MATTHEW POCKET.**

AH!

I *RECOGNISED* THE NAME. IT WAS THE **MATTHEW** WHO WAS TO SIT BY MISS HAVISHAM'S **HEAD**, WHEN SHE **DIED**.

HIS SON IS IN **LONDON** – YOU CAN MEET HIM **FIRST.**

WHEN WILL YOU COME TO LONDON?

STRAIGHT AWAY!

BEFORE YOU DO, YOU WILL NEED NEW **CLOTHES.**

TRAVEL IN ONE WEEK'S TIME.

YOU'LL NEED SOME **MONEY** – SHALL I LEAVE YOU **TWENTY POUNDS?**

CHINK-ERR-CHING!

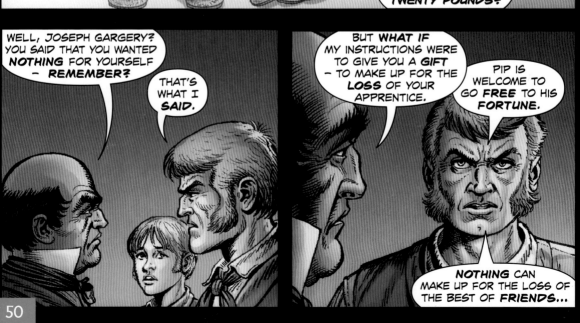

WELL, JOSEPH GARGERY? YOU SAID THAT YOU WANTED **NOTHING** FOR YOURSELF – **REMEMBER?**

THAT'S WHAT I **SAID.**

BUT **WHAT IF** MY INSTRUCTIONS WERE TO GIVE YOU A **GIFT** – TO MAKE UP FOR THE **LOSS** OF YOUR APPRENTICE.

PIP IS WELCOME TO GO **FREE** TO HIS **FORTUNE.**

NOTHING CAN MAKE UP FOR THE LOSS OF THE BEST OF **FRIENDS...**

PIP'S GOING TO BE A **GENTLEMAN** OF FORTUNE – AND GOD **BLESS** HIM!

OH! CONGRATULATIONS!

BIDDY AND JOE WERE IMPRESSED THAT THE MAKER OF MY FORTUNE WAS TO REMAIN **SECRET.** ALL THEY WERE ALLOWED TO SAY WAS THAT I HAD COME INTO GREAT EXPECTATIONS FROM A **MYSTERIOUS** PATRON.

AY, THAT'S **ALL** WE'LL SAY, PIP.

BIDDY TRIED HARD TO MAKE MY SISTER **UNDERSTAND** WHAT HAD HAPPENED.

PIP...

...PROPERTY

I DON'T THINK SHE UNDERSTOOD.

THAT NIGHT, I SAW JOE AND BIDDY OUTSIDE AND HEARD THEM **FONDLY** TALKING ABOUT ME.

THIS FIRST NIGHT OF MY BRIGHT **FORTUNE** WAS THE **LONELIEST** I HAD EVER KNOWN.

EVEN MY OLD BED FELT **UNEASY** NOW, AND I NEVER SLEPT SOUNDLY IN IT AGAIN.

THE NEXT MORNING AFTER BREAKFAST, WE BURNED MY APPRENTICESHIP PAPERS – I WAS *FREE*.

VOLUME I
CHAPTER XIX

AFTER CHURCH, AND AN EARLY DINNER, I WENT FOR A *WALK*.

I WAS *ASHAMED* TO THINK THAT I'D ONCE HELPED A CONVICT HERE – BUT THAT WAS A *LONG* TIME AGO, AND HE WOULD HAVE BEEN TAKEN FAR AWAY. HE WAS *DEAD* TO ME.

I LAY DOWN AND FELL ASLEEP, THINKING ABOUT *MISS HAVISHAM* AND *ESTELLA*.

WHEN I AWOKE, THERE WAS JOE!

I THOUGHT I'D *FOLLOW* YOU.

I'M GLAD YOU DID. YOU KNOW, I'D *ALWAYS* WANTED TO BE A GENTLEMAN.

REALLY?

IT'S A PITY THAT YOU DIDN'T GET ON *BETTER* IN YOUR STUDIES HERE WITH ME, JOE.

WELL, I DON'T KNOW – I'M SO AWFULLY *DULL* – ALL I KNOW IS MY OWN TRADE.

BIDDY, PLEASE **HELP** JOE TO **BETTER** HIMSELF – IN HIS **LEARNING** AND **MANNERS**.

OH! WON'T HIS MANNERS **DO** THEN?

NOT IF HE WAS TO MIX WITH **WEALTHIER** PEOPLE...

HE MAY NOT **WANT** TO MIX WITH WEALTHIER PEOPLE.

I AM VERY **SORRY** TO SEE THIS IN YOU, BIDDY.

YOU ARE **JEALOUS** OF MY **FORTUNE**.

IF YOU **THINK** SO!

I AM **VERY** SORRY TO **SEE** IT – **FORGET** I ASKED YOU TO DO **ANYTHING** FOR JOE.

I ASK **NOTHING** OF YOU.

MISS HAVISHAM BEHAVED LIKE A FAIRY **GODMOTHER** WHO HAD **CHANGED** ME.

I HAVE COME INTO **SUCH** GOOD **FORTUNE**, MISS HAVISHAM; AND I AM SO **GRATEFUL** FOR IT!

MR. JAGGERS TOLD ME **ALL** ABOUT IT, PIP.

GOODBYE, PIP! YOU WILL **ALWAYS** KEEP THE NAME OF PIP, YOU KNOW.

I WORE MY NEW CLOTHES FOR BIDDY AND JOE, AND WE SPENT A **SAD** EVENING TOGETHER.

I WAS TO LEAVE AT FIVE IN THE MORNING, AND I WANTED TO WALK AWAY **ALONE**.

HOOROAR!

I WALKED AWAY QUICKLY, THINKING IT WAS **EASY** TO LEAVE...

...BUT WHEN I THOUGHT OF EVERYTHING I WAS LEAVING **BEHIND**, I BEGAN TO CRY.

I'D COME TOO **FAR** TO GO BACK NOW.

THE WHOLE **WORLD** LAY BEFORE ME.

VOLUME II
CHAPTER I

IT TOOK FIVE HOURS TO REACH LONDON. I WAS SCARED BY THE *SIZE* OF IT; AND EVERYWHERE SEEMED NARROW AND *DIRTY*.

I WAS TO CALL UPON MR. JAGGERS IN *LITTLE BRITAIN.*

IS MR. JAGGERS HERE?

NO – HE'S IN *COURT.*

ARE YOU MR. *PIP?*

YES.

MR. JAGGERS SAID FOR YOU TO *WAIT* FOR HIM IN HIS *ROOM.*

THE ROOM WAS A *DISMAL* PLACE. THERE WERE TWO DREADFUL CASTS OF *FACES* ON THE WALL – I WONDERED WHO THEY *WERE.*

I COULDN'T *BEAR* TO SIT WITH THE FACES FOR LONG, SO I WENT FOR A SHORT WALK. SOON I WAS BY *NEWGATE PRISON.*

THERE, I SAW THE *GALLOWS* WHERE MEN WERE HANGED...

...IT MADE ME *FEEL QUITE SICK.*

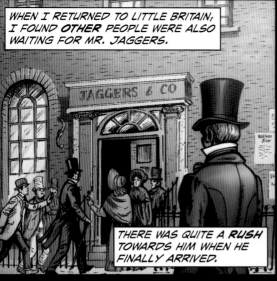

WHEN I RETURNED TO LITTLE BRITAIN, I FOUND **OTHER** PEOPLE WERE ALSO WAITING FOR MR. JAGGERS.

THERE WAS QUITE A **RUSH** TOWARDS HIM WHEN HE FINALLY ARRIVED.

I HAVE **NOTHING** MORE TO SAY TO YOU. FROM THE START, I SAID THERE WAS ONLY A SMALL **CHANCE**.

HAVE YOU **PAID** WEMMICK?

YES, SIR.

WHAT ABOUT MY **HUSBAND**, SIR?

I HAVE TOLD YOU I WILL TAKE **CARE** OF HIM – NOW STOP **BOTHERING** ME, OR I **WON'T** HELP HIM.

HAVE YOU **PAID** WEMMICK?

I HAVE, SIR!

MY GUARDIAN TOOK ME INTO HIS ROOM. HE TOLD ME I WAS TO GO TO "BARNARD'S INN" AND STAY WITH YOUNG MR. POCKET.

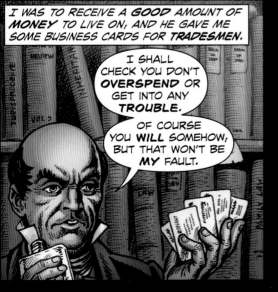

I WAS TO RECEIVE A **GOOD** AMOUNT OF **MONEY** TO LIVE ON, AND HE GAVE ME SOME BUSINESS CARDS FOR **TRADESMEN**.

I SHALL CHECK YOU DON'T **OVERSPEND** OR GET INTO ANY **TROUBLE**.

OF COURSE YOU **WILL** SOMEHOW, BUT THAT WON'T BE **MY** FAULT.

MR. JAGGERS'S CLERK **WEMMICK** TOOK ME TO BARNARD'S INN.

I TELL YOU IT'S NO **USE** – HE WON'T SEE **ANY** OF YOU.

THAT WAS A **LONG** TIME AGO – SORRY FOR HITTING YOU AND **HURTING** YOU SO MUCH.

THAT'S **NOT** HOW **I** REMEMBER IT!

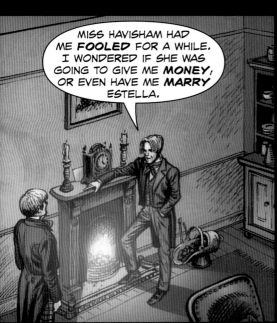

MISS HAVISHAM HAD ME **FOOLED** FOR A WHILE. I WONDERED IF SHE WAS GOING TO GIVE ME **MONEY**, OR EVEN HAVE ME **MARRY** ESTELLA.

WERE YOU DISAPPOINTED?

OH, NO – SHE'S **NASTY**.

MISS HAVISHAM?

NO, **ESTELLA**. SHE HAS BEEN TAUGHT BY MISS HAVISHAM TO MAKE MEN **MISERABLE**.

ARE THEY **RELATED** TO EACH OTHER?

NO, ESTELLA IS **ADOPTED**.

WHY **DOES** SHE DISLIKE MEN?

DEAR ME! DON'T YOU **KNOW?** IT'S QUITE A **STORY** – I SHALL TELL IT TO YOU OVER DINNER.

YOUR GUARDIAN, MR. JAGGERS, IS MISS HAVISHAM'S **SOLICITOR**. I'M GLAD THAT HE SUGGESTED MY FATHER TO BE YOUR **TEACHER**.

MY FATHER IS MISS HAVISHAM'S **COUSIN**, BUT THEY DON'T **TALK** TO EACH OTHER.

I TOLD HIM MY STORY, TELLING HIM HOW I COULDN'T EVEN **TRY** TO FIND OUT WHO MY BENEFACTOR WAS.

AS I WAS RAISED AS A COUNTRY **BLACKSMITH**, PLEASE LET ME KNOW WHENEVER YOU SEE ME BEING **IMPOLITE** OR GETTING THINGS **WRONG**.

OF COURSE.

PLEASE CALL ME **HERBERT**.

MY NAME IS **PHILIP**.

I DON'T **LIKE** THAT NAME. AS YOU WERE A BLACKSMITH, HOW ABOUT I CALL YOU **HANDEL**?

HE WROTE A PIECE OF **MUSIC** CALLED THE HARMONIOUS BLACKSMITH.

I'D LIKE THAT.

THEN, MY DEAR **HANDEL**, HERE IS **DINNER**.

I REMINDED HERBERT ABOUT HIS **PROMISE** TO TELL ME THE STORY OF **MISS HAVISHAM**.

HER MOTHER **DIED** WHEN SHE WAS **YOUNG**, AND HER FATHER **SPOILT** HER. HE WAS A **RICH** BREWER, AND **ALL** HIS MONEY WENT TO **HER**.

DIDN'T SHE HAVE ANY BROTHERS OR SISTERS?

SHE LET THE WHOLE PLACE GO TO **WASTE**, AND HAS NEVER SEEN **DAYLIGHT** SINCE.

THE MAN SHE WAS GOING TO **MARRY** WAS WORKING WITH HER **HALF-BROTHER**, AND THEY **SHARED** THE MONEY HE GOT FROM HER.

WHAT **BECAME** OF THEM?

THEY FELL INTO DEEPER **SHAME** AND **RUIN**.

WE CHANGED THE SUBJECT. HERBERT HAD **PLANS** TO GO INTO **INTERNATIONAL** TRADE.

YOU NEED TO LOOK AROUND YOU TO FIND **OPPORTUNITIES** TO MAKE **MONEY**. AND WHEN YOU MAKE THAT MONEY, ALL YOU NEED TO DO IS **INVEST** IT.

ALREADY IT SEEMED **MONTHS** SINCE I HAD LEFT JOE AND BIDDY.

THE **FOLLOWING** MONDAY AFTERNOON, WE WENT TO MR. MATTHEW POCKET'S HOUSE, IN **HAMMERSMITH**.

BELINDA, I HOPE YOU HAVE **WELCOMED** MR. PIP?

YES...

MRS. POCKET WAS THE DAUGHTER OF A **KNIGHT**, WHO WAS RAISED TO MARRY A MAN OF TITLE – BUT **WITHOUT** TELLING HER FATHER, SHE MARRIED THE UNTITLED MR. POCKET **INSTEAD**.

HE TOOK ME INTO THE HOUSE AND INTRODUCED ME TO TWO OTHER MEN STAYING THERE: **DRUMMLE** AND **STARTOP**.

ALTHOUGH IT WAS MR. AND MRS. POCKET'S HOUSE, I FOUND OUT AT DINNER THAT IT WAS THE **SERVANTS** WHO WERE REALLY IN CHARGE.

WHEN THE PAGE TOLD MR. POCKET THAT THE COOK HAD **LOST** THE **BEEF**, HE WAS SO ANGRY THAT HE TRIED TO LIFT HIMSELF UP BY HIS OWN **HAIR**!

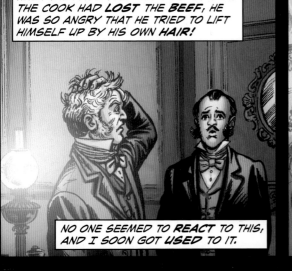

NO ONE SEEMED TO **REACT** TO THIS, AND I SOON GOT **USED** TO IT.

AFTER DINNER, AND A ROW ON THE RIVER, WE LEARNED THAT THE COOK WAS LYING **DRUNK** ON THE KITCHEN **FLOOR**.

AM I **NOTHING** IN THE HOUSE? THE COOK HAS SAID HOW I WAS **BORN** TO BE A **DUCHESS**...

GOODNIGHT, MR. PIP!!!

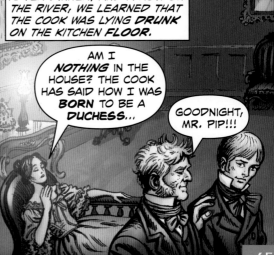

AFTER A FEW DAYS, MR. POCKET AND I DISCUSSED THE DETAILS OF MY **EDUCATION.** I WAS NOT TO BE TAUGHT FOR ANY PARTICULAR PROFESSION, BUT WAS TO BE GROOMED TO BE **COMFORTABLE** IN UPPER SOCIETY.

I WANTED TO **STAY** AT BARNARD'S INN WITH **HERBERT.** MR. POCKET AGREED TO THIS, BUT **FIRST** I NEEDED TO GET **APPROVAL**...

...FROM MY **GUARDIAN.**

IF I COULD BUY SOME **FURNITURE** AND A FEW OTHER THINGS, I SHOULD BE QUITE AT **HOME** THERE.

HOW **MUCH** MONEY DO YOU **WANT?**

HOW MUCH? **FIFTY** POUNDS?

OH, NOT **NEARLY** SO MUCH.

FIVE POUNDS?

OH, MORE THAN **THAT.**

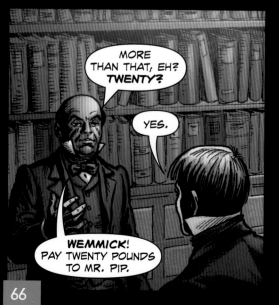

MORE THAN THAT, EH? **TWENTY?**

YES.

WEMMICK! PAY TWENTY POUNDS TO MR. PIP.

MR. JAGGERS WENT **OUT.**

I DON'T KNOW **WHAT** TO MAKE OF MR. JAGGERS'S MANNER.

HE'D BE **PLEASED** TO HEAR THAT!

HE WANTS TO KEEP **EVERYONE** ON THEIR TOES – IT'S PART OF HIS JOB AS A LAWYER.

WHO **ARE** THESE PEOPLE?

THEY'RE FAMOUS CLIENTS — **MURDERERS.**

THE CASTS WERE MADE IN NEWGATE PRISON JUST **AFTER** THEY WERE **HANGED.**

ONE OF THEM BOUGHT THIS FOR ME.

AND THE OTHER ONE GAVE ME THIS **RING** AS A **GIFT** THE DAY BEFORE HE DIED.

DO YOU GET **MANY** GIFTS THAT WAY?

OH **YES,** AND I TAKE THEM. I ALWAYS LIKE TO GET HOLD OF **PORTABLE** PROPERTY.

IF AT ANY TIME YOU WOULD **VISIT** ME AT MY HOME IN WALWORTH, I WOULD CONSIDER IT AN **HONOUR.**

I HAVE TWO OR THREE **THINGS** THERE THAT MIGHT INTEREST YOU.

I'D BE **DELIGHTED** TO.

HAVE YOU **DINED** WITH MR. JAGGERS YET?

NOT YET.

WHEN YOU DO, LOOK AT HIS **HOUSEKEEPER.** YOU'LL SEE A WILD **BEAST** THAT HAS BEEN **TAMED.**

I DIDN'T SEE MR. WEMMICK FOR SOME **WEEKS**, SO I WROTE TO HIM SUGGESTING A VISIT TO HIS HOME. HE WAS **DELIGHTED**, AND WE ARRANGED TO MEET AT THE OFFICE.

I HOPE YOU DON'T **OBJECT** TO MEETING MY AGED PARENT?

NOT AT **ALL**.

INCIDENTALLY, I THINK MR. JAGGERS IS GOING TO INVITE YOU AND YOUR FRIENDS TO **DINNER** TOMORROW.

EVENTUALLY, WE ARRIVED IN THE DISTRICT OF WALWORTH.

PRETTY, ISN'T IT? THAT'S A **REAL** FLAGSTAFF, AND ON **SUNDAYS** I RUN UP A REAL **FLAG**.

AFTER I HAVE CROSSED THIS BRIDGE, I HOIST IT UP, TO CUT MYSELF **OFF** FROM THE **WORLD**.

THE BRIDGE CROSSED A REALLY NARROW TROUGH – BUT HE TOOK GREAT **PRIDE** IN HOISTING IT UP.

I FIRE THIS GUN AT NINE EVERY NIGHT. WHEN YOU HEAR IT, YOU'LL SAY HE'S A **STINGER!**

I LOOK AFTER **EVERYTHING** YOU SEE HERE. IT MAKES A NICE **CHANGE** FROM MY JOB, AND IT **PLEASES** MY FATHER.

LET ME **INTRODUCE** YOU TO HIM.

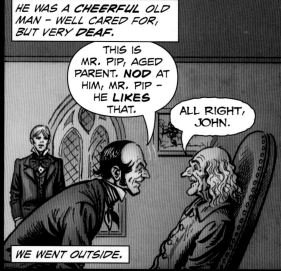

HE WAS A **CHEERFUL** OLD MAN – WELL CARED FOR, BUT VERY **DEAF**.

THIS IS MR. PIP, AGED PARENT. **NOD** AT HIM, MR. PIP – HE **LIKES** THAT.

ALL RIGHT, JOHN.

WE WENT OUTSIDE.

IT HAS TAKEN ME **YEARS** TO BRING THIS HOUSE AND GARDENS UP TO SCRATCH.

DOES MR. JAGGERS LIKE IT?

HE'S NEVER **SEEN** IT. I KEEP MY HOME **SEPARATE** FROM MY WORK.

IT'S GETTING NEAR GUN-FIRE. IT'S THE AGED'S **TREAT**.

THE AGED WAS **HEATING** A POKER FOR THIS NIGHTLY CEREMONY.

JUST BEFORE NINE, WEMMICK TOOK THE RED-HOT POKER UP TO THE BATTERY...

...AND AT THE STROKE OF NINE...

BOOOOOOM

I HEARD HIM!

WEMMICK WAS UP **EARLY** NEXT MORNING.

AFTER BREAKFAST, WE WENT TO LITTLE BRITAIN.

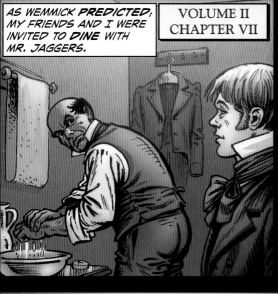

AS WEMMICK **PREDICTED**, MY FRIENDS AND I WERE INVITED TO **DINE** WITH MR. JAGGERS.

VOLUME II
CHAPTER VII

AS SUGGESTED, I TOOK NOTICE OF THE **HOUSEKEEPER**.

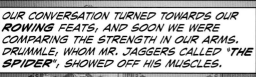

OUR CONVERSATION TURNED TOWARDS OUR **ROWING** FEATS, AND SOON WE WERE COMPARING THE STRENGTH IN OUR ARMS. DRUMMLE, WHOM MR. JAGGERS CALLED "**THE SPIDER**", SHOWED OFF HIS MUSCLES.

MR. JAGGERS **STOPPED** THE HOUSEKEEPER FROM CLEARING THE TABLE AND **GRABBED** HER HANDS.

I'LL SHOW YOU ALL **STRENGTH**. MOLLY, LET THEM SEE YOUR **WRISTS**.

Master, **don't**.

YES, MOLLY – **BOTH** YOUR WRISTS.

THERE'S **POWER** HERE. VERY FEW **MEN** HAVE THIS STRENGTH.

THAT WILL DO, MOLLY – YOU CAN **GO**.

AT HALF-PAST NINE, GENTLEMEN, YOU MUST **LEAVE**.

AND AT HALF-PAST NINE, WE DEPARTED.

A MONTH OR SO LATER, I RECEIVED A LETTER.

My dear Mr. Pip:
Mr. Gargery is going to London and would like to see you.
He will be at Barnard's Hotel Tuesday morning 9 o'clock.
Your poor sister is much the same as when you left.
We talk of you often.
Your affectionate servant,
Biddy.
P.S. he says for me to write What Larks.

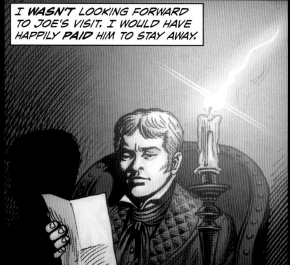

I WASN'T LOOKING FORWARD TO JOE'S VISIT. I WOULD HAVE HAPPILY **PAID** HIM TO STAY AWAY.

I TIDIED OUR ROOMS, AND ON THE TUESDAY MORNING I HEARD JOE ON THE STAIRCASE. I **KNEW** IT WAS JOE BY HIS **CLUMSY** MANNER.

‡tap‡

JOE, HOW ARE YOU, JOE?

PIP, HOW **AIR** YOU, PIP?

I AM GLAD TO **SEE** YOU, JOE.

MY – HOW YOU'VE **GROWED**. YOU ARE A' **HONOUR** TO YOUR KING AND COUNTRY.

YOU LOOK **WONDERFULLY** WELL.

US TWO BEING **ALONE**, SIR...

JOE, **HOW** CAN YOU CALL **ME** SIR?

I WON'T STAY LONG. WELL, **SIR**, I WERE AT THE BARGEMEN T'OTHER NIGHT, WHEN PUMBLECHOOK SAID, "JOSEPH, MISS HAVISHAM SHE WISH TO SPEAK TO YOU."

NEXT DAY, SIR, HAVING CLEANED MYSELF, I GO AND I SEE **MISS A.**

MISS A., JOE? MISS HAVISHAM?

WHICH I SAY, SIR — MISS A., OR OTHERWAYS **HAVISHAM.**

SHE SAID, "MR. GARGERY, WOULD YOU TELL MR. PIP THAT ESTELLA HAS COME HOME AND WOULD BE **GLAD** TO SEE HIM."

THAT'S ME **DONE**, SIR. I WISH YOU EVER **WELL.**

YOU'RE GOING SO **SOON?**

YES.

PIP, DEAR OLD CHAP, YOU AND ME SHOULDN'T BE **TOGETHER** IN LONDON; NOR ANYWHERE **ELSE.**

I'M **WRONG** IN THESE CLOTHES, AND I'M WRONG OUT OF THE **FORGE. GOD BLESS YOU,** DEAR OLD PIP!

AND WITH THAT, HE **LEFT.**

I WOKE IN A **FRIGHT**, WHEN I HEARD HIM SAY...

...TWO ONE POUND NOTES.

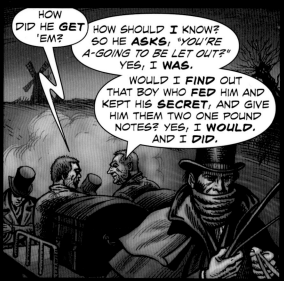

HOW DID HE **GET** 'EM?

HOW SHOULD **I** KNOW? SO HE **ASKS**, "YOU'RE A-GOING TO BE LET OUT?" YES, I **WAS**.

WOULD I **FIND** OUT THAT BOY WHO **FED** HIM AND KEPT HIS **SECRET**, AND GIVE HIM THEM TWO ONE POUND NOTES? YES, I **WOULD**. AND I **DID**.

MORE FOOL **YOU**. I'D HAVE **SPENT** 'EM ON FOOD AND DRINK. HE **KNOWED NOTHING** OF YOU.

NOT A **THING**. DIFFERENT **GANGS** AND DIFFERENT **SHIPS**. HE WAS MADE A **LIFER**.

ALTHOUGH I WAS **AMAZED** TO HEAR THIS, I WAS CERTAIN THAT HE DIDN'T KNOW **WHO** I WAS.

THE CONVICTS CONTINUED ON THEIR WAY WHILE I, FEELING AFRAID, **WALKED** ON TO THE BLUE BOAR.

I WAS UP TOO **EARLY** NEXT MORNING TO GO TO MISS HAVISHAM'S, SO I WALKED AROUND, THINKING ABOUT THE **BRILLIANT PLANS** SHE MUST HAVE FOR ME.

SHE HAD **ADOPTED** ESTELLA, AND AS **GOOD** AS ADOPTED **ME**. SHE MUST WANT US TO BE **TOGETHER**.

I RANG THE BELL AND TURNED MY BACK UPON THE GATE.

ORLICK!

AH, YOUNG MASTER, THERE'S MORE CHANGES THAN **YOURS!**

THEN YOU HAVE **LEFT** THE FORGE?

DOES THIS **LOOK** LIKE THE **FORGE?**

ORLICK **LEFT** ME TO WALK UP TO MISS HAVISHAM'S ROOM IN THE **DARK.**

tap-ta-tap

PIP'S KNOCK! **COME IN,** PIP

SITTING NEAR HER WAS AN ELEGANT LADY WHO I HAD **NEVER** SEEN BEFORE.

SO YOU KISS MY HAND AS IF I WERE A **QUEEN,** EH?

YOU **ASKED** ME TO COME AND SEE YOU, AND I CAME STRAIGHT AWAY.

WELL?

THE **UNKNOWN** LADY LIFTED UP HER EYES...

...AND I SAW IT WAS **ESTELLA.**

SHE WAS SO BEAUTIFUL, THAT I BECAME THE COARSE AND **COMMON** BOY AGAIN.

I -- IT'S A-- P-**PLEASURE** TO S-**SEE** YOU AGAIN.

YOU FIND HER **MUCH** CHANGED, PIP?

I DIDN'T **RECOGNISE** HER AT FIRST --

-- BUT NOW IT ALL SETTLES DOWN INTO THE **OLD** --

WHAT? NOT INTO THE **OLD** ESTELLA! SHE WAS **PROUD** AND **INSULTING** -- REMEMBER?

THAT WAS A **LONG** TIME AGO.

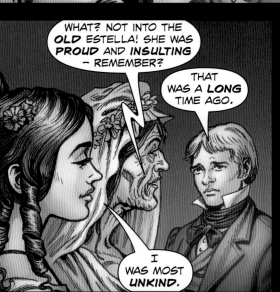

I WAS MOST **UNKIND.**

AFTER A WHILE, THE TWO OF US WALKED IN THE NEGLECTED GARDEN. I WAS **TREMBLING** WITH **ADMIRATION** FOR HER, BUT SHE SHOWED **NO EMOTION** TOWARDS ME.

I TOOK HER TO WHERE SHE HAD **GIVEN** ME MY MEAT AND DRINK.

I DON'T **REMEMBER.**

YOU DON'T **REMEMBER** MAKING ME **CRY?**

NO.

HER NOT **REMEMBERING** OR **CARING** MADE ME CRY **AGAIN**, INSIDE.

YOU MUST **KNOW** THAT I HAVE NO **HEART** AND FEEL NO **EMOTION.**

SOMETHING ABOUT HER FACE SUDDENLY LOOKED **FAMILIAR.** IT WAS **NOT** MISS HAVISHAM -- SO **WHO** WAS IT?

BACK IN THE HOUSE, I FOUND OUT THAT MR. JAGGERS WAS COMING TO **DINNER.** I **WHEELED** MISS HAVISHAM AROUND AS I HAD **YEARS AGO.**

IS SHE **BEAUTIFUL?** DO YOU **ADMIRE** HER?

SURELY, EVERYONE DOES!

LOVE HER!

IF SHE **LIKES** YOU, **LOVE** HER! IF SHE **HURTS** YOU, **LOVE** HER! I **RAISED** HER TO BE LOVED.

LOVE HER!

AAAEEEEEEEEK!

I **CALMED** HER, AND NOTICED THAT MY **GUARDIAN** WAS IN THE ROOM.

MISS HAVISHAM SENT US DOWN TO OUR **DINNER.**

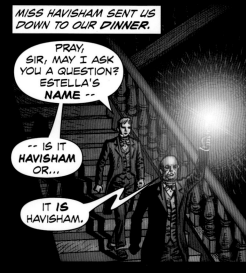

PRAY, SIR, MAY I ASK YOU A QUESTION? ESTELLA'S **NAME** --

-- IS IT **HAVISHAM** OR...

IT **IS** HAVISHAM.

WE PLAYED CARDS AFTER DINNER. IT WAS ARRANGED THAT ESTELLA WAS TO VISIT **LONDON,** AND I WAS TO BE THERE WHEN SHE **ARRIVED.**

BACK AT THE BLUE BOAR, I COULDN'T GET MISS HAVISHAM'S WORDS, **"LOVE HER!"** OUT OF MY HEAD. TO THINK SHE SHOULD BE **DESTINED** FOR **ME,** ONCE A **BLACKSMITH'S BOY!**

I KNEW I MUST **STAY AWAY** FROM **JOE** – ESTELLA DIDN'T **LIKE** HIM OR HIS **COMMON** WAYS.

I FELT IT WAS MY **DUTY** TO **WARN** MR. JAGGERS ABOUT ORLICK.

HE'S NOT THE RIGHT **SORT** OF MAN TO WORK FOR MISS HAVISHAM.

VERY GOOD, PIP. I'LL DISMISS HIM **STRAIGHT AWAY.**

JAGGERS AND I TOOK THE MIDDAY COACH BACK TO LONDON.

MY DEAR HERBERT, I **MUST TELL** YOU SOMETHING.

I **LOVE** – I **ADORE** – ESTELLA.

I KNOW **THAT.**

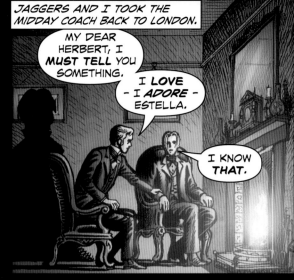

HOW?

WHEN YOU TOLD ME YOUR STORY – YOU SAID YOU **ADORED** HER FROM THE **START.**

IF I ADORED HER **BEFORE**, I NOW **DOUBLY** ADORE HER.

LUCKY FOR **YOU** THEN, THAT MISS HAVISHAM IS GETTING YOU **TOGETHER.**

NOW, HANDEL, I HAVE SOMETHING TO TELL **YOU,** TOO.

I AM SECRETLY **ENGAGED.** HER NAME IS **CLARA.**

SHE IS RATHER **BELOW** WHAT MY MOTHER WANTS FOR ME.

CLARA'S FATHER IS AN **INVALID** WHO STAYS IN AN UPSTAIRS ROOM. I HAVE NEVER **SEEN** HIM --

-- BUT HE SOMETIMES MAKES **SUCH** A **NOISE!** HA, HA, HA!

I SHALL MARRY HER WHEN I HAVE ENOUGH **MONEY.**

THAT NIGHT, WE SAW MR. WOPSLE IN THE THEATRE.

HAMLET PRINCE OF DENMARK

HAYMARKET THEATRE

WAS I TO PLAY **HAMLET** TO MISS HAVISHAM'S **GHOST?**

I am to come to London the day after tomorrow.
Miss Havisham tells me that you are to meet me there.
She sends you her regards.
Yours, Estella.

VOLUME II
CHAPTER XIII

I WENT TO THE COACH-OFFICE *HOURS* BEFORE SHE WAS DUE TO ARRIVE. WHILE THERE, WEMMICK WALKED BY.

HALLOA, MR. PIP. WOULD YOU LIKE TO VISIT *NEWGATE PRISON* WITH ME?

AS HE WORKED FOR MR. JAGGERS, WEMMICK WAS *POPULAR* AMONG THE PRISONERS.

HOW *ARE* YOU, COLONEL?

ALL RIGHT, MR. WEMMICK.

WE DID EVERYTHING WE *COULD*, BUT THE EVIDENCE WAS TOO *STRONG* FOR US.

IT *WAS*, SIR, BUT I AM GLAD TO HAVE THE CHANCE OF SAYING *GOODBYE* TO YOU.

He is sure to be *executed* on Monday.

YOU SILLY BOY, HOW CAN YOU TALK SUCH **NONSENSE?**

MR. POCKET'S FAMILY SEND **BAD** REPORTS ABOUT YOU TO MISS HAVISHAM.

THEY **DESPISE** YOU.

OH, THOSE **PEOPLE!**

IT GIVES ME **GREAT** PLEASURE TO SEE THEM GETTING **NOTHING** FROM HER.

AFTER TEA, WE DROVE AWAY.

WHAT PLACE IS **THAT?**

NEWGATE **PRISON.**

WRETCHES!

WE WERE SOON AT **RICHMOND.**

GOODNIGHT.

HOW **HAPPY** I SHOULD BE TO LIVE HERE WITH HER --

-- YET HOW **MISERABLE** I AM WHEN WE ARE TOGETHER.

81

I STARTED TO NOTICE THAT MY WEALTH, OR "EXPECTATIONS", HAD CHANGED ME – AND NOT FOR THE BETTER.

ALSO, MY LIFESTYLE HAD LED HERBERT INTO EXPENSES THAT HE COULDN'T AFFORD.

WE GRADUALLY FELL FURTHER AND FURTHER INTO DEBT.

MY DEAR HERBERT, WE NEED TO SORT OUT OUR FINANCES.

I WAS LIKE A FIRST-RATE BUSINESSMAN IN THESE SITUATIONS – I KEPT CALM AND MADE GOOD DECISIONS.

slide

IT'S FOR YOU, HANDEL.

THE LETTER WAS FROM TRABB & Cº, TELLING ME THAT MY SISTER, MRS. J. GARGERY, HAD DIED AND THAT HER FUNERAL WAS ON MONDAY NEXT.

I WROTE TO JOE TO **OFFER** MY **SYMPATHY** AND TO TELL HIM THAT I WOULD BE **THERE**.

VOLUME II
CHAPTER XVI

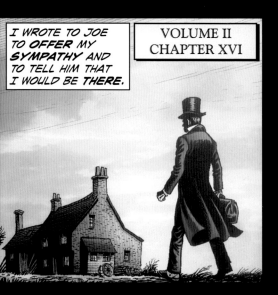

DEAR JOE, HOW **ARE** YOU?

PIP, OLD CHAP, YOU KNEW HER WHEN SHE WAS A **FINE FIGURE** OF A WOMAN.

Here they come!

Here they are!

MY SISTER WAS LAID TO REST CLOSE TO THE GRAVES OF OUR **PARENTS**.

AFTERWARDS, BIDDY, JOE, AND I HAD DINNER TOGETHER. JOE LOOKED UNCOMFORTABLE, BUT HE WAS PLEASED THAT I WANTED TO SLEEP IN MY OLD ROOM.

LATER, BIDDY AND I TALKED OUTSIDE...

I SUPPOSE IT WILL BE DIFFICULT FOR YOU TO STAY HERE NOW, BIDDY?

OH! I CAN'T, MR. PIP.

HOW ARE YOU GOING TO LIVE? IF YOU WANT ANY MO--

I'M APPLYING TO BE THE MISTRESS IN THE NEW SCHOOL NEARBY.

I HAVEN'T HEARD HOW MY SISTER DIED.

SHE HAD BEEN IN A BAD STATE FOR FOUR DAYS. THEN, SHE SUDDENLY SAID, "JOE."

I RAN AND FETCHED MR. GARGERY, AND SHE LAID HER HEAD ON HIS SHOULDER. SHE SAID "JOE" AGAIN, THEN "PARDON," AND THEN "PIP." AN HOUR LATER, SHE WAS GONE.

WHAT HAS HAPPENED TO ORLICK? HAVE YOU SEEN HIM?

I SAW HIM OVER THERE ON THE NIGHT SHE DIED – AND I SAW HIM THERE A MOMENT AGO.

I THINK HE IS WORKING IN THE QUARRIES.

I WAS ANGRY THAT HE WAS STILL FOLLOWING HER.

I'LL DO ALL I CAN TO SEND HIM AWAY.

I CALMED DOWN.

YOU MUST KNOW THAT JOE **LOVES** YOU AND ONLY WANTS THE BEST FOR YOU. HE NEVER **COMPLAINS** ABOUT ANYTHING.

I'LL VISIT HIM **OFTEN** – I WON'T LEAVE POOR JOE **ALONE**.

ARE YOU **SURE** YOU **WILL ACTUALLY** VISIT HIM?

REALLY BIDDY!

I'M **SHOCKED** – DON'T SAY ANOTHER **WORD**.

I KEPT HER AT A **DISTANCE** ALL EVENING.

ALL NIGHT I THOUGHT ABOUT BIDDY'S **INJUSTICE** TOWARDS ME. I LEFT **EARLY** IN THE MORNING.

GOODBYE, DEAR JOE! – I SHALL VISIT **SOON**, AND **OFTEN**.

PLEASE **DO**, PIP.

BIDDY, I AM NOT ANGRY, BUT I AM **HURT**.

DON'T BE – **I'M** THE ONLY ONE WHO SHOULD BE **HURT** IF I HAVE BEEN UNKIND.

THE MISTS WERE RISING AS I WALKED AWAY. BIDDY WAS **RIGHT**...

...I WOULDN'T BE RETURNING SOON.

HERBERT AND I SANK **FURTHER** INTO **DEBT.**

WEEKS PASSED, AND WE EXPECTED MY GUARDIAN TO GIVE ME MORE **INFORMATION** ON MY TWENTY-FIRST BIRTHDAY.

I RECEIVED A NOTE TELLING ME TO VISIT MR. JAGGERS ON THE **DAY** THAT I CAME OF AGE.

I MUST CALL YOU **MR. PIP** TODAY.

CONGRATULATIONS, MR. PIP.

NOW, MY YOUNG FRIEND, DO YOU KNOW HOW **MUCH** YOU ARE **SPENDING?**

NO, SIR.

AS I **THOUGHT!**

NOW, HAVE YOU **ANYTHING** TO ASK **ME?**

MANY THINGS – BUT I AM **FORBIDDEN** TO ASK THEM.

ARE YOU GOING TO TELL ME THE **NAME** OF MY **BENEFACTOR** TODAY?

NO. ASK SOMETHING **ELSE.**

HAVE I ANYTHING TO **RECEIVE,** SIR?

I **THOUGHT** WE SHOULD COME TO IT! YOU HAVE BEEN **OVERSPENDING** AND ARE, NO DOUBT, **HEAVILY** IN **DEBT.**

I AM, SIR.

HERE IS FIVE HUNDRED POUNDS. IT IS A **PRESENT** TO YOU ON THIS DAY. YOU SHALL RECEIVE THIS AMOUNT **EACH** YEAR UNTIL YOUR BENEFACTOR APPEARS.

FROM NOW ON, YOU SHALL LOOK AFTER YOUR **OWN** MONEY AFFAIRS.

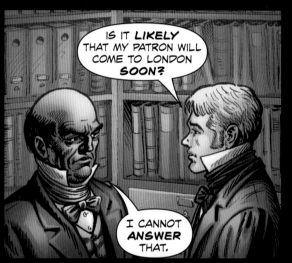

IS IT **LIKELY** THAT MY PATRON WILL COME TO LONDON **SOON?**

I CANNOT **ANSWER** THAT.

I GUESSED THAT MISS HAVISHAM HAD NOT **TOLD** MR. JAGGERS ABOUT HER PLANS FOR **ESTELLA** AND **ME**.

THEN THERE IS NOTHING **MORE** FOR US TO **SAY**. GOOD DAY, SIR.

MR. WEMMICK, COULD YOU **ADVISE** ME PLEASE?

I WANT TO USE MY **MONEY** TO HELP A FRIEND SET UP IN **BUSINESS**.

MR. PIP, YOU MAY AS WELL **THROW** THE MONEY FROM YOUR FAVOURITE BRIDGE INTO THE RIVER **THAMES**.

YOU SHOULD **NEVER** INVEST PORTABLE PROPERTY IN A **FRIEND**.

ON THE NEXT SUNDAY AFTERNOON, I VISITED WEMMICK AT HIS HOME.

HE WAS NOT THERE, SO I *SAT* WITH THE AGED WHILE I *WAITED* FOR HIM TO *RETURN.*

Click

HE'S HOME!

WEMMICK PRESENTED ME TO *MISS SKIFFINS.*

SHE WAS A FREQUENT VISITOR AT THE CASTLE – WEMMICK SHOWED ME ANOTHER FLAP ON HIS INGENIOUS DEVICE WHICH HAD *"MISS SKIFFINS"* ON IT.

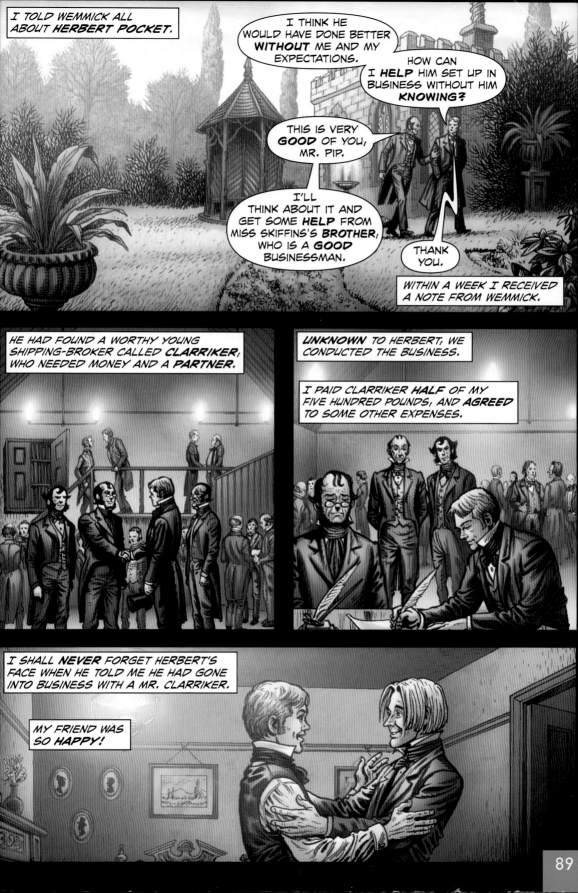

WHEREVER MY BODY WAS, MY **HEART** AND **SPIRIT** WAS WITH **ESTELLA** AT THAT HOUSE IN RICHMOND.

BOTH INSIDE AND OUT OF THAT HOUSE, ESTELLA CONTINUED HER **UNKINDNESS** TOWARDS ME.

THE HOUSE WAS OWNED BY MRS. BRANDLEY, WHO WAS AN **OLD FRIEND** OF MISS HAVISHAM'S.

SHE WOULD **TEASE** ME WITH HER **MANY** ADMIRERS, AND **MAKE FUN** OF MY **DEVOTION** TO HER.

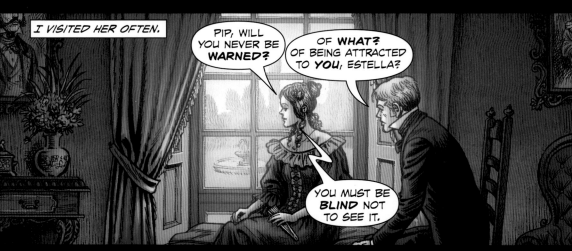

I VISITED HER OFTEN.

PIP, WILL YOU NEVER BE **WARNED?**

OF **WHAT?** OF BEING ATTRACTED TO **YOU**, ESTELLA?

YOU MUST BE **BLIND** NOT TO SEE IT.

MISS HAVISHAM WISHES ME TO **VISIT** HER AT SATIS HOUSE. **YOU** ARE TO TAKE ME **THERE** AND BRING ME **BACK**.

WE WENT, AS **PLANNED**.

MISS HAVISHAM WAS MORE **FOND** OF ESTELLA THAN **EVER**, AND ASKED THE NAMES OF ALL THE **MEN** SHE HAD ATTRACTED.

HOW DOES SHE **USE** YOU, PIP?

I SAW THAT ESTELLA WAS TO WREAK MISS HAVISHAM'S **REVENGE** ON MEN, AND THAT SHE WOULD NOT BE MINE UNTIL HER WORK WAS **DONE**.

FOR THE FIRST TIME, I SAW THEM **ARGUE**.

WHAT! ARE YOU **TIRED** OF ME?

ONLY A LITTLE TIRED OF **MYSELF**.

SPEAK THE **TRUTH** -- YOU **ARE** TIRED OF ME. YOU **COLD**, COLD **HEART!**

YOU **MADE** ME WHAT I AM. TAKE ALL THE **PRAISE**, AND ALL THE **BLAME**.

SO PROUD AND **HARD**, ESTELLA -- BUT NOT TO **ME!**

YOU **TAUGHT** ME TO BE PROUD AND HARD. I HAVE ALWAYS BEEN **FAITHFUL** TO YOUR **SCHOOLING**.

THE **SUCCESS** IS NOT MINE, THE **FAILURE** IS NOT MINE --

-- BUT THE **TWO** TOGETHER **MAKE** ME.

I TOOK MY **CHANCE** TO **LEAVE** THE ROOM.

WHEN I **RETURNED**, EVERYTHING WAS BACK TO **NORMAL**. WE PLAYED CARDS, AS IN YEARS **GONE BY**; AND I WENT TO BED.

NEXT DAY, THERE WAS NO **SIGN** OF ANY **DISAGREEMENT** BETWEEN THEM.

HERBERT AND I JOINED A GENTLEMAN'S CLUB CALLED THE FINCHES OF THE GROVE.

BENTLEY DRUMMLE WAS ALREADY A MEMBER. ONE EVENING, HE WAS CALLED UPON TO TOAST A LADY. I WAS SHOCKED TO HEAR HIM TOAST...

ESTELLA OF RICHMOND!

I **KNOW** HER.

SO DO **I**!

I LEARNED THAT THEY HAD DANCED **TOGETHER** SEVERAL TIMES.

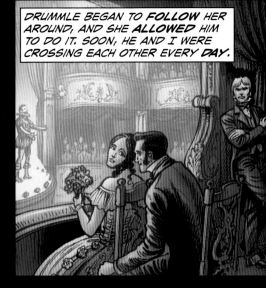

DRUMMLE BEGAN TO **FOLLOW** HER AROUND, AND SHE **ALLOWED** HIM TO DO IT. SOON, HE AND I WERE CROSSING EACH OTHER EVERY **DAY**.

I HAD TO **SPEAK** TO ESTELLA ABOUT HIM.

ESTELLA, **LOOK** AT DRUMMLE OVER THERE IN THE CORNER.

WHAT IS HE TO **ME**?

LET ME **SPEAK**.

NO ONE **LIKES** HIM – AND I HATE TO SEE **YOU** WITH **HIM**.

DON'T BE **FOOLISH**, AND DON'T LET IT **AFFECT** YOU.

DO YOU **DECEIVE** AND **ENTRAP** HIM, ESTELLA?

YES, AND MANY **OTHERS** – **EVERYONE** EXCEPT **YOU**.

I MUST GO, NOW.

I WAS NOW TWENTY-THREE, AND I STILL HADN'T HEARD ANY MORE ABOUT MY **EXPECTATIONS**.

VOLUME II
CHAPTER XX

HERBERT WAS AWAY ON BUSINESS, SO I WAS **ALONE**, READING, WHEN I HEARD **SOMEONE** ON THE **STAIRS**.

≶ CLUMP ≶

THEY **STOPPED** WHEN THEY SAW MY **LAMP**.

WHAT FLOOR DO YOU **WANT?**

THE TOP -- A **MR. PIP.**

I AM **PIP.**

THE STRANGER SEEMED **PLEASED** TO SEE ME.

WHAT DO YOU **WANT?**

LET ME **IN** AND I WILL **EXPLAIN.**

THERE'S NO ONE **ELSE** HERE, IS THERE?

WHY DO YOU, A **STRANGER**, ASK THAT QUESTION?

I'M **GLAD** YOU'VE GROWN UP **STRONG**!

BUT DON'T CATCH **HOLD** OF ME, OR YOU'LL BE **SORRY**.

SUDDENLY, I REALISED...

...I KNEW HIM!

IT WAS MY CONVICT! HE DIDN'T **NEED** TO SHOW ME THE **FILE**.

YOU ACTED **NOBLE**, MY BOY! AND I'VE **NEVER** FORGOT IT!

STAY **AWAY** FROM ME!

IF YOU ARE **GRATEFUL** FOR WHAT I DID THEN I HOPE YOU'VE MENDED YOUR WAYS. BUT YOU MUST **UNDERSTAND** THAT I --

THAT, **WHAT?**

THAT I **CANNOT** BE YOUR **FRIEND**.

I GAVE HIM A *DRINK*. HE SEEMED EMOTIONAL.

I AM SORRY IF I SPOKE *HARSHLY* TO YOU JUST NOW.

HOW HAVE YOU BEEN *LIVING?*

I'VE BEEN LIVING AND WORKING IN *AUSTRALIA.*

HAVE YOU DONE *WELL* THERE?

WONDERFULLY WELL, AND I'M *FAMOUS* FOR IT.

YOU ONCE SENT A *MESSENGER* TO ME WITH TWO ONE-POUND *NOTES.*

TO A *POOR* BOY THEY WERE A SMALL *FORTUNE* – BUT I HAVE *ALSO* DONE *WELL* SINCE THEN, AND YOU *MUST* HAVE THEM *BACK.*

HOW HAVE YOU DONE *WELL*, SINCE WE *MET* ON THE *MARSHES?*

I BEGAN TO *TREMBLE*. I TOLD HIM HOW I WAS GOING TO INHERIT SOME *PROPERTY.*

I FEARED AND DETESTED HIM AS IF HE WERE SOME TERRIBLE BEAST.

I'M YOUR SECOND FATHER, PIP. I'VE PUT AWAY MONEY, SO YOU CAN SPEND IT.

I THOUGHT OF YOU ALL THE TIME I WAS IN AUSTRALIA.

AND I PROMISED, "IF I GETS LIBERTY AND MONEY, I'LL MAKE THAT BOY A GENTLEMAN!" AND I DONE IT.

I'VE LIVED EVERY DAY FOR THIS.

DID YOU EVER THINK IT MIGHT BE ME?

OH NO – NEVER!

WAS THERE NO ONE ELSE?

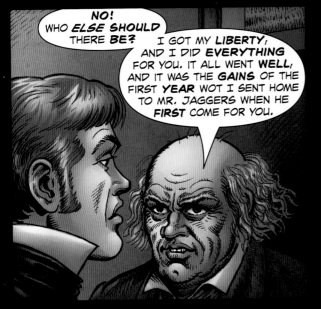

NO! WHO ELSE SHOULD THERE BE? I GOT MY LIBERTY, AND I DID EVERYTHING FOR YOU. IT ALL WENT WELL, AND IT WAS THE GAINS OF THE FIRST YEAR WOT I SENT HOME TO MR. JAGGERS WHEN HE FIRST COME FOR YOU.

IT WARN'T EASY OR SAFE FOR ME TO COME HERE, BUT I STUCK TO IT AND, DEAR BOY, I DONE IT!

WHERE CAN I **SLEEP?** I'VE BEEN AT SEA FOR **MONTHS**.

MY FRIEND IS **AWAY** – YOU CAN HAVE HIS ROOM.

HE WON'T COME BACK **TOMORROW**, WILL HE? WE MUST BE **CAREFUL**. I WAS SENT FOR **LIFE** – AND I'LL BE **HANGED** IF THEY **FIND** ME HERE.

AFTER A SMALL SUPPER HE WENT TO HERBERT'S ROOM. I BEGAN TO REALISE WHAT A **FOOL** I'D BEEN.

MISS HAVISHAM HAD **NO** PLANS FOR ME.

ESTELLA WAS **NOT** DESTINED TO BE MINE.

AND IT WAS FOR THIS **CONVICT** THAT I HAD DESERTED **JOE**.

I SLEPT IN MY **WRETCHEDNESS**...

...WHEN I AWOKE, ALL WAS **DARK** AND **COLD**.

I HAD TO BE **CAREFUL** TO MAKE SURE MY DREADED VISITOR WAS **SAFE.**

I HEARD A NOISE **OUTSIDE...**

WHAT ARE YOU **DOING** THERE?

!?!

WHY WAS THERE A **LURKER** ON THE STAIRS? **TONIGHT** OF ALL **NIGHTS!**

I WENT TO ASK THE WATCHMAN IF HE HAD **LET** ANYONE IN.

ABOUT ELEVEN O'CLOCK, A **STRANGER** ASKED FOR **YOU.**

ERM... MY **UNCLE,** YES.

YOU **SAW** HIM, SIR? AND THE PERSON **WITH** HIM?

PERSON **WITH** HIM?

HE **STOPPED** WHEN YOUR UNCLE TALKED TO ME AND THEN FOLLOWED HIM **INSIDE.**

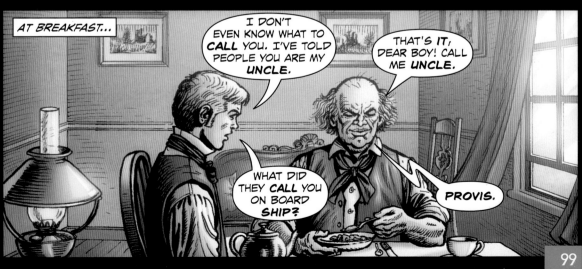

AT BREAKFAST...

I DON'T EVEN KNOW WHAT TO **CALL** YOU. I'VE TOLD PEOPLE YOU ARE MY **UNCLE.**

THAT'S **IT,** DEAR BOY! CALL ME **UNCLE.**

WHAT DID THEY **CALL** YOU ON BOARD **SHIP?**

PROVIS.

I DECIDED IT BEST FOR HIM TO LIVE **CLOSE** BY, AND FOR HIM TO BE THERE WHEN HERBERT **RETURNED**.

ONCE I HAD SECURED SOME NEARBY **LODGING** FOR MY **UNCLE**, MR. PROVIS, I WENT TO LITTLE BRITAIN.

NOW, PIP, BE **CAREFUL**. DON'T TELL ME **ANYTHING** – I DON'T WANT TO **KNOW**.

HE **KNOWS** THE MAN HAS **RETURNED**.

MR. JAGGERS, I MERELY WANT TO MAKE **SURE** THAT WHAT I HAVE BEEN TOLD IS **TRUE**.

YOU SAID **"TOLD"**!

YOU'VE SPOKEN TO HIM DIRECTLY? HOW **CAN** YOU, IF HE'S IN **AUSTRALIA?**

THEN I HAVE BEEN **INFORMED** BY A PERSON NAMED **ABEL MAGWITCH** THAT HE IS MY **BENEFACTOR**.

THAT IS THE **MAN**. IN AUSTRALIA.

AND **ONLY** HE?

ONLY **HE**.

I DON'T HOLD YOU **RESPONSIBLE** FOR MY **MISTAKE**, BUT I ALWAYS THOUGHT IT WAS MISS **HAVISHAM**.

AS YOU SAY, PIP, I AM **NOT** AT **ALL** RESPONSIBLE FOR **THAT**.

WHEN MAGWITCH WROTE TO ME – FROM AUSTRALIA – HE TALKED ABOUT SEEING YOU HERE IN **ENGLAND**. I ADVISED **AGAINST** IT BECAUSE HE WAS SENT AWAY FOR **LIFE**.

WE SHOOK HANDS AND SAID GOODBYE.

THE **FONDER** PROVIS BECAME OF ME, THE MORE I **RECOILED** FROM HIM.

HE WOULD OFTEN ASK ME TO **READ** TO HIM. I EXPECTED HERBERT BACK ANY DAY, SO I **DARED** NOT GO **OUT**.

THIS WENT ON FOR ABOUT **FIVE DAYS**.

ONE EVENING, I HEARD *WELCOME* FOOTSTEPS.

QUIET!

IT'S HERBERT!

HANDEL, MY DEAR FELLOW, HOW **ARE** YOU? I FEEL LIKE I'VE BEEN GONE A **YEAR** OR MORE.

WHY, HANDEL, MY --

-- HALLOA! I BEG YOUR **PARDON.**

HERBERT, MY DEAR FRIEND, SOMETHING VERY **STRANGE** HAS HAPPENED.

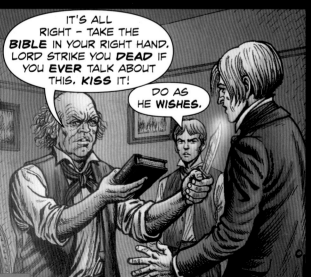

IT'S ALL RIGHT -- TAKE THE **BIBLE** IN YOUR RIGHT HAND. LORD STRIKE YOU **DEAD** IF YOU **EVER** TALK ABOUT THIS. **KISS** IT!

DO AS HE **WISHES.**

NOW YOU'RE UNDER **OATH,** YOU KNOW.

HERBERT WAS *ASTONISHED* TO HEAR THE FULL STORY.

LIKE *ME*, HE FOUND IT *UNPLEASANT* TO BE IN THE SAME ROOM AS MY CONVICT.

I WAS *RELIEVED* WHEN I FINALLY TOOK HIM TO HIS LODGINGS.

WE MUST *DO* SOMETHING. HE WANTS US TO LIVE *EXPENSIVELY*. HE MUST BE *STOPPED*.

THEN YOU *CAN'T* ACCEPT --

HOW *CAN* I? *LOOK* AT HIM!

BUT THE TRUTH IS, HE'S STRONGLY *ATTACHED* TO ME. OH, *CRUEL* FATE!

LOOK HOW MUCH I *OWE* HIM ALREADY – YET I HAVE *NO* EXPECTATIONS.

I HAVE BEEN BRED FOR *NO* REASON.

I AM FIT FOR *NOTHING*!

WE MUST GET HIM *OUT* OF *ENGLAND*. YOU GO WITH HIM, AND THEN ESCAPE BACK *HERE*.

WE'LL GET THROUGH THIS *TOGETHER*.

NEXT MORNING, HE TOLD US HIS *STORY*...

IN JAIL AND OUT OF JAIL, IN JAIL AND OUT OF JAIL – THAT'S *MY LIFE*, PRETTY MUCH.

I'VE HAD NEARLY *EVERYTHING* DONE TO ME – EXCEPT BEING *HANGED*. I'VE BEEN PUT OUT OF TOWN, STUCK IN THE STOCKS, EVEN *WHIPPED*.

I DID A BIT OF *EVERYTHING* – TRAMPING, BEGGING, THIEVING, *WORKING* WHEN I *COULD*.

AT EPSOM RACES, OVER *TWENTY* YEARS AGO, I MET A MAN I *HATE* TODAY – *COMPEYSON*. THAT'S WHO I WAS *FIGHTING* ON THE *MARSHES*.

WE BECAME *PARTNERS*. HE USED TO *SWINDLE* – FORGE BANK NOTES AND SUCH-LIKE.

HE HAD *ANOTHER* PARTNER, CALLED *ARTHUR*, WHO GOT *ILL*.

COMPEYSON'S *WIFE* LOOKED AFTER HIM.

THEY'D GOT *MONEY* OUT OF A *RICH LADY* SOME *YEARS* BEFORE, BUT HAD *SPENT* IT ALL.

I WAS ALWAYS IN *DEBT* TO THAT COMPEYSON AND ALWAYS GETTING INTO *TROUBLE* FOR HIM. HE WAS YOUNGER AND *SMARTER* THEN ME.

ME AND MY *MISSIS*, ERR --

HE *PAUSED* AND LOOKED *CONFUSED*.

NO MATTER ABOUT **THAT.**

IN THE END WE WERE **CAUGHT.** WE WERE TRIED **SEPARATELY.** I SOLD **EVERYTHING** I HAD TO GET **JAGGERS** TO DEFEND ME.

ALL THE EVIDENCE WENT AGAINST **ME,** NOT **HIM.** COMPEYSON WAS GIVEN **MERCY** FOR **GOOD** CHARACTER AND **BAD** COMPANY. I WAS FOUND **GUILTY.**

HE GOT **SEVEN** YEARS, I GOT **FOURTEEN.**

I TOLD HIM, "WHEN I GET CHANCE, I'LL **SMASH** THAT FACE OF YOURN!"

I FINALLY **GOT HIM** ON THE PRISON SHIP.

I WAS PUT IN THE BLACK-HOLE, BUT I **ESCAPED** TO THE SHORE – AND I WAS **HIDING** AMONG THE GRAVES THERE, WHEN I FIRST SAW MY **BOY!**

HE TOLD ME THAT COMPEYSON WAS OUT ON THEM MARSHES, **TOO.** I HUNTED HIM DOWN AND SMASHED HIS **FACE.**

I WAS **CAUGHT,** PUT IN **IRONS** AND SENT AWAY FOR **LIFE.** I DIDN'T **STOP** FOR LIFE, THOUGH, 'CAUSE I'M BACK HERE **NOW.**

HERBERT SECRETLY PUSHED A **BOOK** TO ME THAT HE'D BEEN **WRITING** IN.

Young Havisham's name was Arthur.

Compeyson must have been Miss Havisham's lover.

The BOOK Common and Admi of SACRA and other monies ac UNITED Toge

VOLUME III
CHAPTER IV

I DIDN'T TELL **PROVIS** ABOUT **ESTELLA**. I WENT TO **RICHMOND** TO SEE HER, BUT SHE HAD GONE TO VISIT MISS HAVISHAM.

SHE HAD **NEVER** GONE THERE WITHOUT ME **BEFORE.**

NEXT DAY, I SET OFF FOR MISS HAVISHAM'S. WHEN I GOT TO THE BLUE BOAR, **THERE** WAS **BENTLEY DRUMMLE**!

THIS IS A **BEASTLY** PLACE --

-- **YOU'RE** FROM ROUND HERE, AREN'T YOU?

YES -- I AM TOLD IT IS **VERY** LIKE WHERE YOU'RE FROM.

NOTHING LIKE IT. LOTS OF **MARSHES** HERE -- AND **ODD** LITTLE PUBLIC-HOUSES AND BLACKSMITHS.

HE CALLED TO THE WAITER, WITH A LOOK OF **TRIUMPH** ON HIS FACE.

IS THAT HORSE OF MINE **READY?**

HURRY UP, SIR. I'M GOING TO DINE AT THE **LADY'S** TONIGHT.

MR. DRUMMLE, I DID NOT **WANT** TO TALK TO YOU, AND DON'T WISH TO TALK TO YOU **EVER** AGAIN.

ME **NEITHER** -- BUT DON'T LOSE YOUR **TEMPER.**

HAVEN'T YOU LOST **ENOUGH** ALREADY WITHOUT LOSING **THAT** TOO?

WE SAT IN **SILENCE** UNTIL HE FINALLY LEFT.

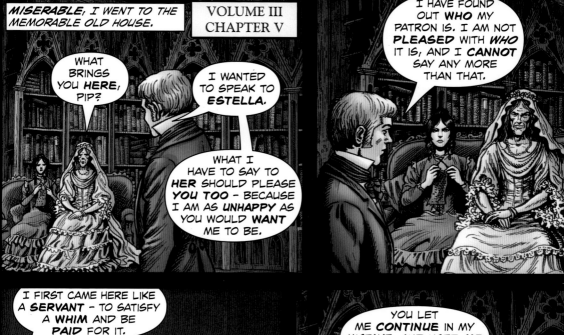

MISERABLE, I WENT TO THE MEMORABLE OLD HOUSE.

WHAT BRINGS YOU **HERE**, PIP?

I WANTED TO SPEAK TO **ESTELLA**.

WHAT I HAVE TO SAY TO **HER** SHOULD PLEASE **YOU TOO** – BECAUSE I AM AS **UNHAPPY** AS YOU WOULD **WANT** ME TO BE.

I HAVE FOUND OUT **WHO** MY PATRON IS. I AM NOT **PLEASED** WITH **WHO** IT IS, AND I **CANNOT** SAY ANY MORE THAN THAT.

I FIRST CAME HERE LIKE A **SERVANT** – TO SATISFY A **WHIM** AND BE **PAID** FOR IT.

MR. **JAGGERS** --

MR. JAGGERS HAD **NOTHING** TO DO WITH IT. YOUR PATRON AND I HAVE THE SAME **LAWYER** – THAT'S **ALL**.

YOU LET ME **CONTINUE** IN MY MISTAKE, AND USED **ME** TO PUNISH YOUR **OWN** RELATIONS.

I **DID**. BUT YOU MADE YOUR OWN **TRAPS**. I NEVER **MADE** THEM.

I MUST TELL YOU THAT YOU DEEPLY **WRONG** MR. MATTHEW POCKET AND HIS SON HERBERT. THEY ARE **GOOD** PEOPLE.

WHAT DO YOU **WANT** FOR THEM?

FOR YOU TO BE **KIND** TO THEM.

ALSO, THAT YOU WOULD SPARE THE **MONEY** TO HELP HERBERT IN BUSINESS.

I **STARTED**, BUT FOR REASONS I CANNOT EXPLAIN, I AM UNABLE TO **CONTINUE**.

WHAT **ELSE?**

ESTELLA, YOU **KNOW** I LOVE YOU.

I HAD **HOPED** THAT MISS HAVISHAM **MEANT** US FOR EACH OTHER --

-- BUT NOW I KNOW THE TRUTH, I **MUST** SAY THIS.

I KNOW WE SHALL **NEVER BE TOGETHER**, ESTELLA. **STILL,** I LOVE YOU.

I HAVE LOVED YOU EVER SINCE I **FIRST** SAW YOU IN THIS HOUSE.

WHEN YOU SAY YOU **LOVE** ME, I KNOW THE **WORDS,** BUT NOTHING **MORE.** I DON'T **FEEL** ANYTHING IN MY **HEART.**

I HAVE ALREADY WARNED YOU HOW I DON'T FEEL **ANY** EMOTION.

I HAD HOPED YOU DIDN'T **MEAN** IT – BEAUTIFUL ESTELLA!

IT IS MY **NATURE** – I CANNOT **HELP** IT.

IS IT NOT **TRUE** THAT BENTLEY DRUMMLE IS HERE FOR **YOU?**

YOU **CANNOT** LOVE HIM! YOU WOULD NEVER **MARRY** HIM, ESTELLA?

YES – I **AM** GOING TO MARRY HIM.

I STAYED AT COVENT GARDEN. WRETCHED AND **WEARY**, I WONDERED WHY I COULD NOT GO **HOME**.

EARLY NEXT MORNING, I WENT TO SEE WEMMICK.

HALLOA, MR. PIP! YOU CAME **BACK**, THEN. CAN YOU TOAST THIS **SAUSAGE** FOR THE AGED P.?

YES, OF COURSE.

NOW, MR. PIP. I ACCIDENTALLY **HEARD** YESTERDAY MORNING – IT'S BEST NOT TO MENTION **NAMES** – THAT A CERTAIN PERSON HAD **DISAPPEARED** FROM A CERTAIN **FAR-OFF** COUNTRY.

I ALSO HEARD THAT YOU HAD BEEN **WATCHED** – I CAN'T SAY BY **WHOM**.

HAVE YOU HEARD OF A MAN OF BAD CHARACTER, WHOSE TRUE NAME IS **COMPEYSON**? IS HE **LIVING**? IS HE IN **LONDON**?

WEMMICK **NODDED SILENTLY.**

NOW – LET ME TELL YOU WHAT I **DID**. I COULDN'T FIND YOU, SO I WENT TO **CLARRIKER'S** TO FIND MR. **HERBERT**.

I TOLD HIM THAT **ANY** STRANGER OR VISITOR SHOULD BE **KEPT** OUT OF **SIGHT**, BUT NOT **TOO** FAR OUT OF THE WAY.

MR. HERBERT CAME UP WITH A **PLAN**. HE MENTIONED TO ME THAT HE IS COURTING A YOUNG LADY WHO LIVES NEAR TO THE RIVER.

HER HOUSE HAS A SPARE **ROOM** WHERE SOMEONE COULD **STAY** OUT OF SIGHT.

THEN, IT WOULD BE **EASY** FOR THIS PERSON TO HURRY ON BOARD A SHIP **LEAVING** ENGLAND.

IN A FEW HOURS, MR. HERBERT HAD ARRANGED **EVERYTHING** – AND NOW I'VE DONE ALL I **CAN** DO.

THANK YOU FOR YOUR **HELP**.

YOU ARE VERY **WELCOME**.

I MUST BE OFF – YOU SHOULD STAY **HERE** UNTIL TONIGHT.

I SOON FELL **ASLEEP** BY THE FIRE, AND LEFT WHEN IT WAS QUITE **DARK**.

ALL IS **WELL**, HANDEL. HE IS **EAGER** TO SEE YOU.

YOU **MUST** MEET CLARA. SHE IS WITH HER **FATHER** AT THE MOMENT.

BANG BANG! BANG BANG! AARGH!

THUMP

THAT'S HER FATHER, NOW. HE IS A SAD OLD **RASCAL**, BUT I HAVE NEVER **SEEN** HIM. I DON'T KNOW HOW CLARA WOULD **COPE** WITHOUT THE HELP OF MRS. WHIMPLE. CLARA'S **ONLY** RELATIVE IS OLD **GRUFFANDGRIM**.

SURELY, THAT'S NOT HIS **NAME**!

NO, NO — HIS NAME IS MR. BARLEY.

THE DOOR OPENED, AND A VERY PRETTY GIRL CAME IN. HERBERT, **BLUSHING**, INTRODUCED ME TO **CLARA**.

SHE WAS TRULY LOVELY AND CHARMING. I WAS SO **HAPPY** FOR HERBERT.

HERBERT AND I WENT TO SEE PROVIS. HE SEEMED **CALMER** THAN WHEN WE FIRST MET.

I TOLD HIM WHAT WEMMICK HAD SAID ABOUT BEING **WATCHED**, AND ABOUT GETTING HIM **ABROAD**.

WHEN THE **TIME** COMES, I WILL GO **WITH** YOU.

WE CAN TAKE HIM DOWN THE RIVER **OURSELVES**.

WE SHOULD KEEP A **BOAT** AND GET INTO THE HABIT OF **ROWING** UP AND DOWN. SOON, NO ONE WILL **NOTICE** US.

WE ALL **LIKED** THIS IDEA. PROVIS WAS TO **WATCH** FOR US ON THE RIVER AND **SIGNAL** TO US WITH HIS WINDOW BLIND.

I ROSE TO LEAVE.

I DON'T LIKE TO **LEAVE** YOU HERE, BUT IT'S **SAFER** THIS WAY. **GOODBYE**!

I DON'T **KNOW** WHEN WE WILL MEET AGAIN, BUT I DON'T **LIKE** GOODBYE. SAY **GOODNIGHT**!

GOODNIGHT! I'LL BE **READY** WHEN THE **TIME** COMES.

I SOON SET ABOUT TRAINING IN OUR NEW BOAT – SOMETIMES **ALONE**, AND SOMETIMES WITH **HERBERT**.

PROVIS **SIGNALLED** TO US AS WE ROWED BY.

STILL, I FELT THAT WE WERE BEING **WATCHED**.

WEEKS PASSED WITHOUT ANY **SIGN** FROM WEMMICK.

I DECIDED NOT TO TAKE ANY MORE **MONEY** FROM MY PATRON, AND HAD TO SELL **JEWELLERY** TO RAISE **CASH**.

PLEDGE TOKENS

5/-

ESTELLA WOULD HAVE BEEN **MARRIED** BY NOW. I BEGGED HERBERT NEVER TO **SPEAK** ABOUT HER.

IT WAS AN **UNHAPPY** LIFE THAT I LIVED – OVER MANY DAYS I ROWED MY BOAT...

...**WAITING** AS BEST I COULD.

LATE FEBRUARY, I WENT TO SEE **MR. WOPSLE** IN A PLAY.

IT IS THE **STRANGEST** THING – YOU'LL HARDLY **BELIEVE** IT!

YOU REMEMBER ONE CHRISTMAS DAY WHEN YOU WERE A **CHILD** AND WE CHASED AFTER TWO **CONVICTS?**

YES.

WELL, THE ONE WHO HAD BEEN **HIT** SAT **BEHIND** YOU TONIGHT!

I WAS **TERRIFIED** AT THE THOUGHT OF **COMPEYSON** BEING LIKE A **GHOST** BEHIND ME.

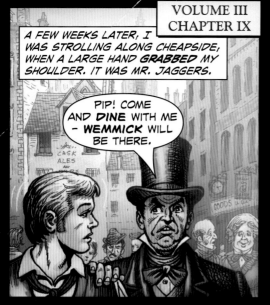

A FEW WEEKS LATER, I WAS STROLLING ALONG CHEAPSIDE, WHEN A LARGE HAND GRABBED MY SHOULDER. IT WAS MR. JAGGERS.

PIP! COME AND DINE WITH ME – WEMMICK WILL BE THERE.

MISS HAVISHAM TELLS ME SHE WANTS TO DISCUSS SOME BUSINESS WITH YOU. WHEN WILL YOU SEE HER?

I SHALL GO TOMORROW.

SO, PIP! OUR FRIEND THE SPIDER HAS PLAYED HIS CARDS. HE HAS WON ESTELLA – BUT HE MAY NOT HAVE IT ALL HIS OWN WAY.

HE MAY BE STRONGER, BUT SHE IS SMARTER.

SO, HERE'S TO MRS. BENTLEY DRUMMLE! MAY THE RESULT BE TO THE LADY'S SATISFACTION!

MOLLY, HOW SLOW YOU ARE TODAY!

SHE LOOKED NERVOUS. SOMETHING IN HER EYES, HER HANDS AND HER FLOWING HAIR LOOKED FAMILIAR.

I LOOKED AGAIN AND REMEMBERED HOW I FELT WHEN I SAW A CERTAIN FACE AT A STAGE-COACH WINDOW AND LATER IN A CARRIAGE PASSING NEWGATE PRISON.

I WAS CERTAIN THAT THIS WOMAN WAS ESTELLA'S MOTHER.

WEMMICK AND I LEFT EARLY TOGETHER.

DO YOU REMEMBER TELLING ME TO NOTICE THAT **HOUSEKEEPER**? A WILD **BEAST** TAMED, YOU CALLED HER.

HOW DID MR. JAGGERS **TAME** HER?

THAT'S HIS **SECRET**. SHE HAS BEEN WITH HIM FOR **MANY** YEARS.

DO **YOU** KNOW HER STORY?

ABOUT TWENTY YEARS AGO, MR. JAGGERS DEFENDED HER IN A **MURDER** TRIAL.

IT WAS A CASE OF **JEALOUSY**. THE MURDERED WOMAN WAS LARGER AND MUCH **STRONGER** THAN MR. JAGGERS'S HOUSEKEEPER.

SHE WAS KILLED BY **CHOKING**.

THEY **SAID** THAT MOLLY WAS **SO** JEALOUS THAT SHE HAD KILLED HER OWN **CHILD** TO **SPITE** HER HUSBAND.

BUT SHE **DRESSED** IN A WAY THAT MADE HER LOOK **WEAKER** THAN SHE WAS, AND **UNABLE** TO STRANGLE ANYONE.

SHE LIVED **ROUGH** AND HAD MARRIED **UNOFFICIALLY** AT A YOUNG AGE.

THERE WASN'T ENOUGH **EVIDENCE** AGAINST HER, AND SHE WAS SET **FREE**.

SHE WENT TO **WORK** FOR MR. JAGGERS STRAIGHT AWAY.

WAS HER CHILD A **BOY** OR A **GIRL**?

A **GIRL**.

I WENT HOME WITH **MUCH** TO THINK ABOUT.

I WAS **SHOCKED** WHEN SHE STARTED TO **WEEP** AT MY FEET.

-- AND REPLACED IT WITH **ICE**.

IT WOULD BE **BETTER** TO TRY TO PUT RIGHT WHAT YOU HAVE **DONE** --

WHAT HAVE I **DONE**!

BELIEVE ME, PIP ⸵sob⸵ ALL I WANTED WAS ⸵sob⸵ TO **SAVE** HER FROM **MISERY** ⸵sob⸵ LIKE MY **OWN**.

BUT GRADUALLY, AS SHE GREW, I **STOLE** HER HEART AWAY --

-- THAN TO GO ON REGRETTING THE **PAST**.

MAY I ASK YOU A **QUESTION** ABOUT **ESTELLA?**

GO ON.

WHOSE CHILD WAS SHE?

I DON'T **KNOW.** I HAD BEEN SHUT UP IN THESE ROOMS A **LONG** TIME, WHEN I TOLD MR. JAGGERS THAT I WANTED TO **RAISE** A LITTLE **GIRL** AND SAVE HER FROM **MY** FATE.

I CALLED HER **ESTELLA.**

SHE WAS TWO OR THREE YEARS OLD WHEN I **ADOPTED** HER.

WE PARTED. IT WAS GETTING **DARK** WHEN I WENT DOWNSTAIRS. I DECIDED TO HAVE ONE LAST WALK AROUND THE OLD PLACE.

AGAIN, IN THE OLD BREWERY, I IMAGINED I SAW MISS HAVISHAM *HANGING* FROM A BEAM...

...BUT IT WAS JUST A *TRICK* OF THE LIGHT.

I DECIDED TO GO *BACK* UPSTAIRS TO *CHECK* THAT SHE WAS ALL RIGHT.

SHE WAS SITTING AS I HAD *LEFT* HER, CLOSE TO THE *FIRE*.

AAAARRRRRRRGGGGGGHHHHH!!!

I SMOTHERED THE **FLAMES** WITH MY **COAT**.

I ALSO USED THE ROTTEN TABLECLOTH.

CLANK!

CHINK!

121

SHE HAD PASSED OUT. I SENT FOR HELP AND *HELD* HER UNTIL IT *ARRIVED.*

BOTH OF MY HANDS WERE BADLY *BURNT.*

THE SURGEON SAID SHE HAD BEEN BADLY HURT, BUT THE MAIN *DANGER* TO HER WAS *SHOCK.*

I COULD BE OF NO FURTHER *HELP,* SO I DECIDED TO *LEAVE* WHEN MORNING CAME.

AS I LEANED OVER HER, SHE SAID...

Write under my name, "I Forgive her."

BACK AT OUR CHAMBERS, HERBERT LOOKED AFTER ME.

IS ALL **WELL** DOWN THE RIVER?

YES — I SAT WITH PROVIS LAST NIGHT, AND HE TOLD ME **MORE** ABOUT HIS LIFE. YOU REMEMBER HE STARTED TO TALK ABOUT A **WOMAN**?

WELL, THIS WOMAN HAD A VERY **JEALOUS** NATURE — JEALOUS TO THE **LAST** DEGREE.

TO **WHAT** LAST DEGREE?

MURDER!

VOLUME III
CHAPTER XI

SHE WAS **TRIED** FOR IT AND MR. **JAGGERS** DEFENDED HER. THE VICTIM WAS A STRONGER WOMAN, FOUND **STRANGLED** IN A BARN. THERE WASN'T ENOUGH **EVIDENCE** AGAINST HER AND SHE WAS SET FREE. THIS JEALOUS WOMAN AND PROVIS HAD A **CHILD** WHO HE DEEPLY **LOVED.**

ON THE NIGHT OF THE MURDER SHE TOLD HIM SHE WOULD **DESTROY** THE CHILD, AND HE WOULD NEVER SEE IT AGAIN.

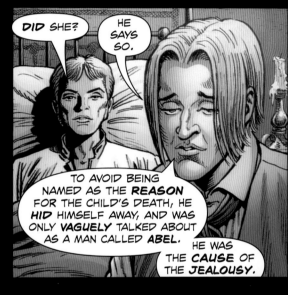

DID SHE?

HE SAYS SO.

TO AVOID BEING NAMED AS THE **REASON** FOR THE CHILD'S DEATH, HE **HID** HIMSELF AWAY, AND WAS ONLY **VAGUELY** TALKED ABOUT AS A MAN CALLED **ABEL.** HE WAS THE **CAUSE** OF THE **JEALOUSY.**

DID HE SAY **WHEN** ALL THIS HAPPENED?

ABOUT **TWENTY** YEARS AGO.

HERBERT! THE MAN WE HAVE **HIDING** DOWN BY THE RIVER --

-- IS **ESTELLA'S FATHER!**

I'M NOT SURE **WHY** I WAS SO KEEN TO ESTABLISH ESTELLA'S **TRUE** PARENTAGE.

EARLY NEXT MORNING, I WENT TO LITTLE BRITAIN AND FOUND MR. JAGGERS AND WEMMICK GOING OVER THE OFFICE ACCOUNTS.

I PRODUCED MISS HAVISHAM'S **AUTHORITY** TO RECEIVE THE NINE HUNDRED POUNDS FOR HERBERT. MR. JAGGERS TOLD WEMMICK TO ISSUE THE **CHEQUE** FOR THE MONEY.

I AM SORRY THAT WE DO NOTHING FOR **YOU**, PIP.

ALL I ASKED OF MISS HAVISHAM WAS TO GIVE ME SOME **INFORMATION** ABOUT ESTELLA'S **ADOPTION**.

I NOW KNOW **MORE** ABOUT ESTELLA THAN MISS HAVISHAM – I KNOW HER **MOTHER**.

MOTHER?

YOU HAVE SEEN HER MORE **RECENTLY** THAN I HAVE.

I KNOW HER **FATHER** TOO.

I COULD TELL THAT MR. JAGGERS **DIDN'T** KNOW WHO THE FATHER WAS.

REALLY?

YES, AND HIS NAME IS **PROVIS** – FROM **AUSTRALIA**

MR. JAGGERS WAS **SHOCKED** BY THIS.

DOES HE HAVE ANY **EVIDENCE?**

NO – HE DOESN'T **EVEN KNOW** THAT HIS DAUGHTER IS STILL **ALIVE**.

PIP, LET ME PUT A **CASE** TO YOU. MIND, I DON'T **ADMIT** ANYTHING HERE.

LET'S SAY THAT THERE WAS A WOMAN WHO KEPT HER **CHILD** HIDDEN AWAY; AND LET'S SAY THAT HER LEGAL ADVISER NEEDED TO **FIND** A CHILD FOR AN ECCENTRIC RICH LADY TO **ADOPT**.

GO ON.

LET'S SAY THAT THE ADVISER **REGULARLY** SAW CHILDREN OF CONVICTS BEING **NEGLECTED**, **IMPRISONED** AND **ABUSED**.

AND LET'S SAY THAT THIS PRETTY CHILD COULD BE **SAVED**, WHERE THE FATHER BELIEVED HER **DEAD** AND THE WOMAN WAS **CLEARED**.

I UNDERSTAND.

THEN LET'S SAY THAT THE **WOMAN** WAS **CALMED** BY HER ORDEAL AND WENT TO THE ADVISER FOR **SHELTER**.

FINALLY, LET'S SAY THAT THE CHILD GREW UP AND **MARRIED**.

THE MOTHER AND THE FATHER WERE STILL ALIVE, AND, **UNKNOWN** TO ONE ANOTHER, LIVING **CLOSE** TO EACH OTHER.

ALL THESE FACTS BEING HELD **SECRET**.

THEN **WHO** WOULD **BENEFIT** FROM THE SECRET BEING **REVEALED?**

NOW, WEMMICK, WHERE **WERE** WE WHEN MR. PIP CAME IN?

MR. JAGGERS AND WEMMICK WENT BACK TO WORK AS **REFRESHED** AS IF THEY HAD JUST HAD **LUNCH**.

125

I WENT TO GET THE **PASSPORTS**, WHILE HERBERT ORGANISED THINGS WITH **STARTOP**.

WHEN I GOT HOME, I FOUND A GRUBBY **LETTER** THAT HAD BEEN **DELIVERED** BY **HAND**...

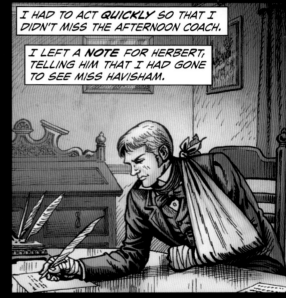

I HAD TO ACT **QUICKLY** SO THAT I DIDN'T MISS THE AFTERNOON COACH.

I LEFT A **NOTE** FOR HERBERT, TELLING HIM THAT I HAD GONE TO SEE MISS HAVISHAM.

> IF YOU ARE NOT AFRAID TO COME TO THE MARSHES TONIGHT OR TOMORROW NIGHT AT NINE, COME TO THE SLUICE-HOUSE BY THE LIMEKILN. IF YOU WANT INFORMATION REGARDING YOUR UNCLE PROVIS, YOU HAD BETTER COME AND TELL NO ONE. YOU MUST COME ALONE.
>
> BRING THIS WITH YOU.

I WENT TO SATIS HOUSE AND WAS TOLD THAT MISS HAVISHAM WAS TOO **ILL** TO SEE ME.

I COULDN'T **FIND** THE **LETTER** BUT I KNEW THE **DETAILS** – SO I HURRIED OFF TO THE **MARSHES**.

THE LIGHTS OF THE DISTANT **PRISON SHIPS** WERE **BEHIND** ME, AS I WALKED TOWARDS THE SLUICE-HOUSE.

I **OPENED** THE DOOR...

CREEEEEAK...

NOW I'VE **GOT** YOU!

HELP, HELP!

LET ME **GO!**

WHY HAVE YOU ATTACKED ME IN THE **DARK?**

BECAUSE I WORK **ALONE.** **ONE** PERSON KEEPS A **SECRET** *BETTER* THAN **TWO.**

DO YOU KNOW **WHERE** I GOT THIS GUN? YOU **COST** ME THAT PLACE, **AND** YOU CAME BETWEEN ME AND A YOUNG **WOMAN** I **LIKED.**

YOU **ALWAYS** GAVE OLD ORLICK A **BAD** NAME.

YOU GAVE IT TO **YOURSELF.** WHAT ARE YOU GOING TO **DO** TO ME?

I'M GOING TO HAVE YOUR **LIFE!** I'LL PUT YOUR **BODY** IN THE **KILN** SO NO ONE'LL FIND **ANYTHING** OF YOU.

IT'S **YOUR** FAULT WOT I DID TO YOUR **SISTER.** YOU WERE **FAVOURED,** AND I WAS BULLIED AND **BEAT.** NOW YOU'RE GOING TO **PAY.**

:gulp:
:gulp:

I'LL TELL YOU SOMETHING **MORE.** IT WAS OLD ORLICK AS YOU TUMBLED OVER ON YOUR **STAIRS** THAT NIGHT. WHY WAS I **THERE?** I'VE BEEN WATCHING YOU, AND I **FOUND** YOUR UNCLE PROVIS!

BUT YOU DON'T **HAVE** AN UNCLE --

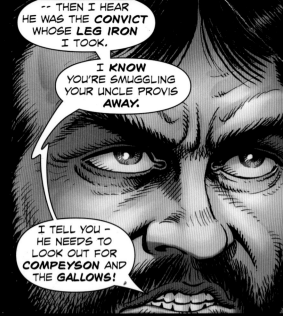

-- THEN I HEAR HE WAS THE **CONVICT** WHOSE **LEG IRON** I TOOK.

I **KNOW** YOU'RE SMUGGLING YOUR UNCLE PROVIS **AWAY.**

I TELL YOU -- HE NEEDS TO LOOK OUT FOR **COMPEYSON** AND THE **GALLOWS!**

HE FINISHED HIS **BOTTLE,** AND PICKED UP A **STONE-HAMMER.**

AARRG GHHH!!

GASP!

HA!

!

AARRR!!

129

WHEN I WOKE UP, THERE WAS TRABB'S BOY!

I THINK HE'LL BE ALL RIGHT.

HERBERT!

AND STARTOP!

MY DEAR HANDEL – CAN YOU **STAND?**

YES, I CAN **WALK** – IT'S JUST MY **ARM.**

IT WAS **BADLY** HURT.

HERBERT TOLD ME HOW I HAD DROPPED THE LETTER IN OUR **CHAMBERS.** TRABB'S BOY HAD **SHOWN** THEM THE WAY TO THE SLUICE-HOUSE.

WE GAVE UP ON THE IDEA OF **FINDING** ORLICK SO THAT WE COULD RETURN TO **LONDON...**

...AND GET READY TO TAKE **PROVIS** AWAY.

I SPENT THE DAY IN BED – MY ARM AND HEAD WERE VERY **PAINFUL.**

EVENTUALLY, I FELL ASLEEP.

WEDNESDAY MORNING I FELT MUCH BETTER. HERBERT, STARTOP AND I PREPARED TO CARRY OUT OUR **PLAN**.

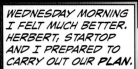

WE WOULD ROW PROVIS **OUT** OF LONDON UNTIL **DARK** AND STAY THE NIGHT IN A TAVERN, **WAITING** FOR THE **STEAMERS** TO COME BY ON THURSDAY MORNING.

WELL **DONE**, DEAR BOY!

THANKYE, **THANKYE**!

I MADE SURE WE WEREN'T BEING **FOLLOWED**, WHILE MY FRIENDS ROWED WITH A STEADY STROKE.

WE CONTINUED **AFTER** NIGHTFALL AND CAME TO A **LONELY** PUBLIC HOUSE WHERE WE **STAYED** THE NIGHT.

WE WERE UP **EARLY** AND ROWED OUT INTO THE TRACK OF THE **STEAMER.**

AS IT APPROACHED, WE GOT READY AND SAID OUR **GOODBYES.**

SUDDENLY, A **GALLEY** APPEARED FROM THE RIVER BANK.

THE HAMBURG STEAMER WAS ALMOST UPON US, WHEN THE GALLEY **HAILED:**

YOU HAVE A RETURNED TRANSPORTED **CONVICT** THERE.

HIS NAME IS ABEL **MAGWITCH,** SOMETIMES CALLED **PROVIS.**

HE MUST **SURRENDER.**

I WAS **UNDER** FOR A WHILE...

...BUT MANAGED TO GET BACK TO THE **SURFACE**. OUR BOAT, AND THE CONVICTS, HAD **GONE**.

FINALLY, I SPOTTED **MAGWITCH**.

:gasp:

SPLAASHH!

WE NEVER **FOUND** COMPEYSON.

MAGWITCH HAD BEEN **INJURED**. HE WHISPERED TO ME THAT HE HAD **STRUCK** COMPEYSON WHILE THEY WERE BOTH UNDERWATER.

HE WAS **BADLY** HURT. HE WOULD RECEIVE **ROUGH** TREATMENT FOR **RETURNING** FROM AUSTRALIA AND **KILLING** ANOTHER.

IT WAS PROBABLY **BEST** THAT HE SHOULD **DIE**.

I TOLD HIM I WAS **SAD** THAT HE HAD COME HOME FOR **MY** SAKE.

I TOOK MY **CHANCE**. NOW, IT'S **BEST** THAT A **GENTLEMAN** SHOULDN'T BE SEEN WITH **ME**.

I WON'T **LEAVE** YOU. I'LL BE AS **TRUE** TO YOU, AS YOU WERE TO **ME**.

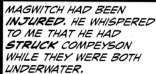

The SHIP

I WAS ALLOWED TO GO BACK **WITH** HIM TO **LONDON**.

I NO LONGER **DISLIKED** HIM. I ONLY SAW A MAN WHO HAD INTENDED TO BE MY **BENEFACTOR**.

HE DIDN'T NEED TO **KNOW** THAT HIS HOPES OF MAKING ME **RICH** HAD **FAILED**.

HIS **TRIAL** WAS DELAYED WHILE THEY SENT FOR AN OLD OFFICER OF THE PRISON-SHIP TO **IDENTIFY** HIM.

I WENT TO MR. JAGGERS FOR **HELP**, BUT HE SAID THERE WAS NO **HOPE** FOR A **DEFENCE**.

WHEN **CONVICTED**, EVERYTHING MAGWITCH **OWNED** WOULD BE **TAKEN** FROM HIM. WE AGREED THAT HE **SHOULDN'T** BE **TOLD** THIS.

IT WAS A **SAD** TIME.

MY DEAR HANDEL, I SHALL SOON HAVE TO **LEAVE** YOU, TO GO TO **CAIRO**. WILL YOU CONSIDER **WORKING** WITH ME THERE?

CAN YOU LEAVE THAT OFFER **OPEN** FOR A LITTLE WHILE?

FOR AS LONG AS YOU **LIKE**!

A FEW DAYS LATER, I SAID **GOODBYE** TO HERBERT. RETURNING TO MY **LONELY** HOME, I FOUND **WEMMICK**.

IT'S A TERRIBLE **WASTE** – THE LOSS OF SO **MUCH** PORTABLE PROPERTY.

I FEEL **MORE** SORRY FOR THE POOR **OWNER**.

TO BE SURE – BUT COMPEYSON WOULD HAVE **FINISHED** HIM OFF ANYWAY.

I HOPE YOU DON'T BLAME **ME**, MR. PIP?

NOT AT **ALL** – I AM FOREVER **GRATEFUL** FOR YOUR FRIENDSHIP.

I AM TAKING A **HOLIDAY** ON MONDAY, MR. PIP. WILL YOU JOIN ME FOR AN EARLY **WALK**?

OF COURSE.

EARLY MONDAY MORNING, WE SET OFF...

HALLOA! HERE'S A CHURCH! LET'S GO IN!

HERE'S SOME GLOVES! LET'S PUT 'EM ON!

I SUSPECTED THAT WEMMICK HAD A PLAN...

...WHICH BECAME OBVIOUS WHEN THE AGED APPEARED WITH MISS SKIFFINS.

HALLOA! HERE'S A RING! LET'S HAVE A WEDDING.

WHO GIVETH THIS WOMAN TO BE MARRIED TO THIS MAN?

NOW AGED P, WHO GIVETH?

ALL RIGHT, JOHN, MY BOY!

WE HAD AN EXCELLENT BREAKFAST AT A PLEASANT LITTLE TAVERN. I DRANK TO THE NEW COUPLE, TO THE AGED, AND TO THE CASTLE.

REMEMBER, MR. PIP, THAT THIS IS A PRIVATE MATTER.

I UNDERSTAND. I WON'T MENTION IT TO MR. JAGGERS.

I DON'T WANT HIM THINKING THAT MY BRAIN HAS GONE SOFT!

MAGWITCH HAD TWO **BROKEN** RIBS AND A **WOUNDED** LUNG. HE WAS FINDING IT DIFFICULT TO **BREATHE**.

THEY MOVED HIM TO THE INFIRMARY, WHERE IT WAS **EASIER** FOR ME TO VISIT HIM.

EACH **DAY** HE GREW **WORSE**.

THE TRIAL WAS VERY **SHORT**. IT WAS **IMPOSSIBLE** TO FIND HIM ANYTHING **OTHER** THAN **GUILTY**.

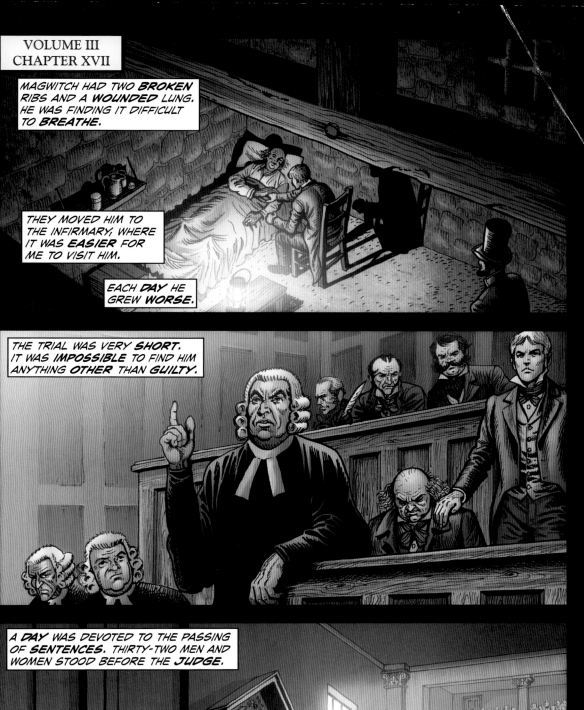

A **DAY** WAS DEVOTED TO THE PASSING OF **SENTENCES**. THIRTY-TWO MEN AND WOMEN STOOD BEFORE THE **JUDGE**.

THE JUDGE ADDRESSED THEM **ALL**, BUT SINGLED OUT ONE WHO HAD BEEN AN OFFENDER SINCE **CHILDHOOD**, AND HAD RETURNED FROM **EXILE**.

I SLEPT VERY LITTLE FOR **SEVERAL** NIGHTS AFTERWARDS. MY DAILY VISITS WERE **SHORTER** NOW THAT HE WAS **GUARDED**.

TEN DAYS **AFTER** THE SENTENCE, I SAW AN EVEN GREATER **CHANGE** IN HIM.

THE APPOINTED **PUNISHMENT** IS **DEATH**.

MY LORD, I HAVE RECEIVED MY SENTENCE OF DEATH FROM THE **ALMIGHTY**, BUT I BOW TO **YOURS**.

HIS HEALTH GREW **WORSE**.

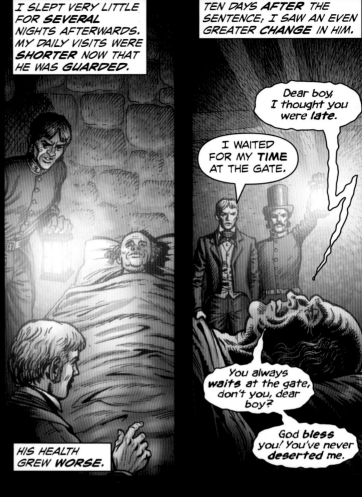

*Dear boy, I thought you were **late**.*

I WAITED FOR MY **TIME** AT THE GATE.

*You always **waits** at the gate, don't you, dear boy?*

*God **bless** you! You've never **deserted** me.*

ARE YOU IN **MUCH** PAIN TODAY?

*I don't **complain** of none, dear boy.*

YOU **NEVER** COMPLAIN.

HE HAD SPOKEN HIS **LAST** WORDS. HE **SMILED** AT ME.

I WAS ALLOWED TO **STAY** A LITTLE LONGER.

I WAS IN **DEBT**,
I HAD NO **MONEY**,
AND I WAS FALLING **ILL**.

**VOLUME III
CHAPTER XVIII**

ONE MORNING,
I COULDN'T **GET UP**.

SOON AFTER, LIKE IN A **DREAM**,
I SAW TWO MEN **LOOKING** AT ME.

WHO ARE YOU?
WHAT DO YOU
WANT?

YOU'RE
UNDER **ARREST** –
FOR **DEBT.**

THEY LET ME **STAY** IN MY **BED.**
I HAD A STRONG **FEVER**, AND I SOON
LOST ALL **SENSE** AND **REASON.**

ONE DAY...

JOE??

I'M HERE,
OLD CHAP.

HOW
LONG HAVE I
BEEN **ILL?**

A WHILE, PIP.
WE GOT **WORD** OF YOU
BEING ILL, AND BIDDY SAID
FOR ME TO COME HERE
RIGHT AWAY.

140

WE TALKED **MORE** NEXT DAY. HE **SHOOK** HIS **HEAD** WHEN I ASKED IF MISS HAVISHAM HAD **RECOVERED.**

IS SHE **DEAD,** JOE?

WHY YOU SEE, OLD CHAP, I WOULDN'T SAY **THAT;** BUT SHE AIN'T **LIVING.**

WHAT WILL BECOME OF HER **HOUSE** AND **POSSESSIONS?**

MOST TO MISS **ESTELLA,** BUT ALSO **FOUR THOUSAND POUNDS** TO MR. MATTHEW **POCKET,** *"BECAUSE OF PIP'S ACCOUNT OF HIM."*

AND OLD ORLICK'S IN **JAIL** FOR BREAKING INTO PUMBLECHOOK'S **HOUSE.**

JOE LOOKED AFTER ME; **SLOWLY,** I GREW **STRONGER.**

WE LOOKED FORWARD TO THE DAY WHEN I WAS **WELL** ENOUGH TO GO **OUTSIDE. THAT** DAY FINALLY CAME...

I AM **GRATEFUL** FOR BEING **ILL,** JOE.

DEAR OLD PIP, YOU'RE **MUCH** BETTER NOW.

I'LL **NEVER FORGET** THIS TIME TOGETHER.

NEXT MORNING, JOE HAD **GONE.** THERE WAS A **BRIEF** LETTER:

not Wishful to intrude I have depArted fur you are well agaiN Dear Pip and will do bEtter without Jo.

P.s. Ever the bEst of friends.

ALONG WITH THE LETTER WAS A **RECEIPT.** JOE HAD **PAID OFF** ALL MY **DEBTS.**

I DECIDED TO GO TO THE **FORGE.** I WOULD SHOW BIDDY HOW MUCH I HAD **CHANGED.** THEN I WOULD **SAY** TO HER:

BIDDY, YOU **LIKED** ME WHEN I WAS **UNWORTHY.**

NOW THAT I AM **WORTHIER,** WILL **YOU** GO THROUGH THE **WORLD** WITH **ME?**

IT SEEMED THAT **EVERYONE** HAD HEARD ABOUT MY MISFORTUNES.

I NO LONGER RECEIVED THE **BEST** ROOM AT THE BLUE BOAR; BUT I STILL SLEPT WELL.

EARLY IN THE MORNING, I WALKED BY SATIS HOUSE. ALL WAS **LOCKED**. THE HOUSE AND FURNITURE WERE TO BE **SOLD** AT **AUCTION**.

Saturday 3ʳᵈ May
FOR SALE BY PUBLIC
AUCTION
SATIS HOUSE

WHEN I GOT BACK TO THE BLUE BOAR, MR. **PUMBLECHOOK** WAS TALKING WITH THE LANDLORD.

YOUNG MAN, I AM SORRY TO SEE YOU BROUGHT SO **LOW**. IT WAS TO BE **EXPECTED**! ARE YOU GOING TO **JOSEPH**?

WHAT DO **YOU** CARE?

FOR ONCE, YOU ARE **RIGHT**. AND THIS IS HIM AS I HAVE SEEN BROUGHT UP BY **HAND**.

WITH THOSE WORDS, HE **LEFT**, SHAKING HIS HEAD.

I WENT TO THE **FORGE** AND SAW JOE AND BIDDY STANDING **ARM-IN-ARM**. BIDDY GAVE A **CRY** AND WAS QUICKLY IN MY **EMBRACE**.

HOW **SMART** YOU **BOTH** ARE!

YES, DEAR PIP.

IT'S MY **WEDDING DAY**, AND I AM **MARRIED** TO **JOE**!

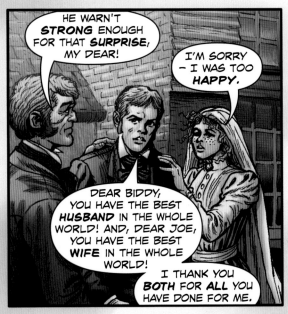

HE WARN'T **STRONG** ENOUGH FOR THAT **SURPRISE**, MY DEAR!

I'M SORRY – I WAS TOO **HAPPY**.

DEAR BIDDY, YOU HAVE THE BEST **HUSBAND** IN THE WHOLE WORLD! AND, DEAR JOE, YOU HAVE THE BEST **WIFE** IN THE WHOLE WORLD!

I THANK YOU **BOTH** FOR **ALL** YOU HAVE DONE FOR ME.

I AM GOING **ABROAD** AND WILL NOT REST UNTIL I HAVE REPAID THE MONEY TO YOU.

BUT I MUST SAY **MORE**.

DEAR JOE, I HOPE YOU WILL HAVE **CHILDREN** TO **LOVE**, AND THAT SOME LITTLE FELLOW WILL ONE DAY **SIT** WITH YOU, AS **I** ONCE DID.

DON'T TELL HIM MY **BAD** POINTS --

-- ONLY TELL HIM THAT I HONOURED YOU **BOTH** BECAUSE YOU WERE SO **GOOD** AND **TRUE**.

AND NOW, PLEASE SAY YOU **FORGIVE** ME.

OH DEAR PIP, GOD KNOWS AS I **FORGIVE** YOU, IF I HAVE **ANYTHING** TO FORGIVE!

ME, **TOO!**

I **SOLD** ALL I HAD, AND WENT TO WORK IN **CAIRO**.

I WAS LEFT IN **CHARGE** OF THE OFFICE WHILE HERBERT WENT **HOME** TO **MARRY CLARA**.

I WAS **HAPPY** THERE AND WROTE **OFTEN** TO BIDDY AND JOE.

WHEN I BECAME A **PARTNER** IN THE FIRM, HERBERT WAS TOLD ABOUT MY **SECRET GIFT** TO HIM. HE WAS **MOVED** AND **AMAZED**.

ELEVEN YEARS LATER, I VISITED JOE AND BIDDY.

THERE, SITTING ON MY OLD LITTLE STOOL, I SAW MYSELF.

WE CALLED HIM PIP AFTER YOU, DEAR OLD CHAP.

BIDDY, YOU MUST LET ME LOOK AFTER HIM ONE DAY.

NO, NO, YOU MUST MARRY.

I DON'T THINK I EVER SHALL, BIDDY.

DEAR PIP, DO YOU STILL FRET FOR HER?

NOT ANY MORE.

THEN HAVE YOU FORGOTTEN ABOUT HER?

NOT FORGOTTEN – BUT THAT DREAM HAS ALL GONE.

EVEN AS I SAID THOSE WORDS, I KNEW THAT I WOULD VISIT THE SITE OF THE OLD HOUSE ONE LAST TIME FOR ESTELLA'S SAKE.

I HAD HEARD THAT ESTELLA WAS UNHAPPY. SHE HAD SEPARATED FROM HER CRUEL HUSBAND.

HE HAD SINCE DIED IN AN ACCIDENT INVOLVING A HORSE HE MISTREATED.

IN THE **COLD** MIST, I SAW A **SOLITARY** FIGURE...

PIP!

ESTELLA!

I'M SURPRISED YOU **RECOGNISE** ME.

THE **FRESHNESS** OF HER BEAUTY HAD GONE, BUT ITS **CHARM** REMAINED.

IT'S **STRANGE** THAT WE SHOULD MEET **HERE,** AFTER ALL THESE **YEARS.**

POOR, **POOR** OLD **PLACE!**

THE **GROUND** BELONGS TO ME – IT'S THE **ONLY** THING I **KEPT.**

RECENTLY, I HAVE OFTEN **THOUGHT** OF YOU.

I REMEMBER WHAT I **THREW AWAY,** THINKING IT WAS **WORTHLESS** --

-- BUT NOW I HAVE GIVEN IT A **PLACE** IN MY **HEART.**

YOU HAVE **ALWAYS** HELD YOUR **PLACE** IN **MY** HEART.

I DIDN'T THINK I WOULD BE LEAVING **YOU** WHEN I LEFT **HERE** — BUT I AM **GLAD** TO.

GLAD TO PART **AGAIN**, ESTELLA? PARTING IS **PAINFUL** TO ME.

BUT YOU ONCE SAID TO ME, "GOD **BLESS YOU**, GOD **FORGIVE YOU!**" --

-- AND IF YOU COULD SAY THAT TO ME **THEN**, YOU CAN SAY IT **NOW**. I HAVE BEEN BENT AND **BROKEN**, BUT — I HOPE — INTO A **BETTER** SHAPE.

BE AS **GOOD** TO ME AS YOU ONCE **WERE**, AND TELL ME WE ARE **FRIENDS**.

WE **ARE** FRIENDS.

AND WILL **CONTINUE** FRIENDS APART.

I TOOK HER HAND IN **MINE**, AND WE LEFT THE **RUINED PLACE**.

AS THE EVENING MISTS ROSE, I SAW NO SHADOW OF ANOTHER **PARTING** FROM HER.

GREAT EXPECTATIONS

The End

Editor's Note:

The last phrase is taken from the revised ending that Dickens wrote for the first single-volume edition of 1862. It is intentionally ambiguous — probably more so than the previously published version of the phrase, which was, "I saw the shadow of no parting from her." However, because Dickens himself obviously felt that the 1862 ending was an improvement, we felt justified to use that phrase for this adaptation.

Charles Dickens

(1812 - 1870)

Charles Dickens was born was born in Landport, Portsmouth, on 7th February 1812. He was the second of eight children born to John and Elizabeth Dickens. Financially, the Dickens family were comfortable, and when they moved to Chatham, Kent in 1817 they sent Charles to the fee paying William Giles' school in the area.

By the time he was ten, the family had moved again; this time to London following the career of his father, John, who was a clerk in the Naval Pay Office. John got into debt and was eventually sent to Marshalsea Prison in 1824. His wife and most of the children joined him there (a common occurrence in those days); Charles, however, was put to work at Warren's Blacking Factory, where he labelled jars of boot polish.

When John's mother died soon after, she left enough money to pay off the debts and reunite the family. Although brief, Charles's time at the factory haunted him for the rest of his life:

> "For many years, when I came near to Robert Warren's, in the Strand, I crossed over to the opposite side of the way, to avoid a certain smell of the cement they put upon the blacking corks, which reminded me of what I once was. My old way home by the borough made me cry, after my oldest child could speak."

Charles Dickens

Charles left school at fifteen and worked as an office boy with a Mr. Molloy of Lincoln's Inn. It was here that Charles made the decision to become a journalist. He studied shorthand at night, and went on to spend two years as a shorthand reporter at the Doctors' Commons Courts.

From 1830 to 1836 he wrote for a number of newspapers; he also started to achieve recognition for his own written work. In December 1833 his first published (but unpaid for) story, *A Dinner at Poplar Walk*, appeared in *The Old Monthly* magazine. About seeing his first work in print, Dickens wrote:

> "On which occasion I walked down to Westminster-hall, and turned into it for half an hour, because my eyes were so dimmed with joy and pride, that they could not bear the street, and were not fit to be seen there".

He wrote further stories for *The Old Monthly*; but when the magazine could not pay for them, Dickens began to write his "series" for *The Chronicle* at the request of the editor, George Hogarth.

In 1835, Charles got engaged to George Hogarth's eldest daughter, Catherine. They married on 2nd April 1836 and went on to have ten children (seven boys and three girls). Biographers have long suspected that Charles preferred Catherine's sister, Mary, who lived with the Dickens family and died in his arms in 1837 at the age of seventeen. Dickens had asked to be buried next to her; but when her brother died in 1841, Dickens's "place" was taken. He wrote to his great friend and biographer John Forster:

"It is a great trial for me to give up Mary's grave… the desire to be buried next to her is as strong upon me now, as it was five years ago… And I know…that it will never diminish…I cannot bear the thought of being excluded from her dust".

The first series of *Sketches by Boz* was published in 1836 ("Boz" was an early pen name used by Dickens). Shortly afterwards, with the success of *Pickwick Papers* in 1837, Dickens was at last a full-time novelist. He produced works at an incredible rate; and at the start of his writing career, also managed to continue his work as a journalist and editor. He began his next book, *Oliver Twist*, in 1837 and continued it in monthly parts until April 1839.

Dickens visited Canada and the United States in 1842. During that visit he talked on the need for international copyright, because some American publishers were printing his books without his permission and without making any payment; he also talked about the need to end slavery. His visit and his opinions were recorded and published as *American Notes* in October of that year, causing quite a stir.

On 17th December 1843 his much-loved Christmas tale, *A Christmas Carol* (also available as a Classical Comics graphic novel) was published. It was so popular that it sold five-thousand copies by Christmas Eve — and has never been out of print since.

From childhood, Dickens had loved the stage and enjoyed the attention and applause he received. He performed in amateur theatre throughout the 1840s and 50s, and formed his own amateur theatrical company in 1845, which occupied much of his time.

Dickens became something of an international celebrity. In 1853 he toured Italy, and on his return to England, he gave the first of many public readings from his own works. At first he did these for charity, but before long he demanded payment.

By 1856, Dickens had made enough money to purchase a fine country house: Gads Hill in Kent. Although he had admired this place ever since his arrival to the area as a child, it was not to be a happy family home. A year later, Charles met a young actress called Ellen Lawless Ternan who went on to join his theatre company; and they began a relationship that was to last until his death.

Charles separated from his wife Catherine in 1858. The event was talked about in the newspapers, and Dickens publicly denied rumours of an affair. He was morally trapped — he was deeply in love with Ellen, but his writing career was based on promoting family values and being a good person; he felt that if he admitted his relationship with Ellen, it would put an end to his career.

Catherine moved to a house in London with their eldest son Charles, and Dickens remained at Gads Hill with the rest of the children and Catherine's sister, Georgina (there were rumours of Charles and Georgina having a relationship, too).

The more he tried to hide his personal life, the more it came out in his writing. *Great Expectations* was written around this time (1860) and includes elements of all the emotions he was experiencing: imprisonment, love that can never be, people living in isolation, and the compulsion to better oneself. He continued to look after Ellen

and made regular secret journeys to see her — not easy for the local celebrity that Dickens had become. He went to incredible lengths to keep his secret safe, including renting houses under different names and setting up offices for his business in places that made it easy for him to visit her.

In 1865, Dickens was involved in the Staplehurst Rail Crash: an incident which disturbed him greatly. He was travelling with Ellen and her mother, most likely returning from a secret holiday in France. The train left the track, resulting in the deaths of ten people and injuries to forty more. It is reported that Dickens tended to some of the wounded.

By 1867 Dickens's health was getting worse. His doctor advised him to rest, but he carried on with his busy schedule, which included a second tour of America.

He returned to England and, despite his bad health, continued his work and his public reading appearances. In April 1869, he collapsed during a reading at

Preston, and he was again advised to rest. Dickens didn't listen. He continued to give performances in London and he even started work on a new novel, *The Mystery of Edwin Drood*. This novel was never finished: he suffered a stroke and died suddenly at Gads Hill on 9th June 1870. He had asked to be buried "in an inexpensive, unostentatious, and strictly private manner" but public opinion, led by *The Times* newspaper, insisted that he should be buried in keeping with his status as a great writer. He was buried at Westminster Abbey on 14th June 1870.

His funeral was a private affair, attended by just twelve mourners. After the service, his grave was left open and thousands of people from all walks of life came to pay their respects and throw flowers onto the coffin. Today, a small stone with a simple inscription marks his grave:

"CHARLES DICKENS
BORN 7th FEBRUARY 1812
DIED 9th JUNE 1870"

The Dickens Family Tree

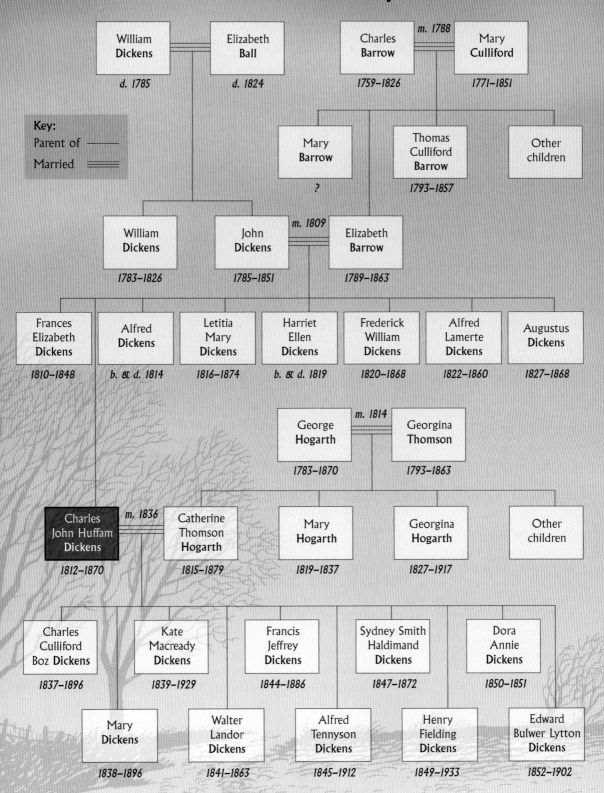

Key:
Parent of ——
Married ═══

William Dickens d. 1785	**Elizabeth Ball** d. 1824	**Charles Barrow** 1759–1826 — m. 1788	**Mary Culliford** 1771–1851

Mary Barrow ?

Thomas Culliford Barrow 1793–1857

Other children

William Dickens 1783–1826

John Dickens 1785–1851 — m. 1809 — **Elizabeth Barrow** 1789–1863

Frances Elizabeth Dickens 1810–1848

Alfred Dickens b. & d. 1814

Letitia Mary Dickens 1816–1874

Harriet Ellen Dickens b. & d. 1819

Frederick William Dickens 1820–1868

Alfred Lamerte Dickens 1822–1860

Augustus Dickens 1827–1868

George Hogarth 1783–1870 — m. 1814 — **Georgina Thomson** 1793–1863

Charles John Huffam Dickens 1812–1870 — m. 1836 — **Catherine Thomson Hogarth** 1815–1879

Mary Hogarth 1819–1837

Georgina Hogarth 1827–1917

Other children

Charles Culliford Boz Dickens 1837–1896

Kate Macready Dickens 1839–1929

Francis Jeffrey Dickens 1844–1886

Sydney Smith Haldimand Dickens 1847–1872

Dora Annie Dickens 1850–1851

Mary Dickens 1838–1896

Walter Landor Dickens 1841–1863

Alfred Tennyson Dickens 1845–1912

Henry Fielding Dickens 1849–1933

Edward Bulwer Lytton Dickens 1852–1902

Due to the lack of official records of births, deaths and marriages within this period, the above information is derived from extensive research and is as accurate as possible from the limited sources available.

Crime and Punishment

A strong thread of criminality runs throughout *Great Expectations*, much as it did in everyday Victorian London. Dickens himself was of course no stranger to the "wrong side of the law". As a young man, his father served time as an insolvent debtor in Marshalsea Prison, and for a while Charles worked as a court reporter. He also lived in a time of great social change, brought about by the increase in population, the impact of technological advances, the rise of industry, and the development of travel and transportation; but unfortunately also an increase in crime.

Elizabeth Fry

The most notable prison reformer of the nineteenth century was Elizabeth Fry. Born in Norwich in 1780, she decided while still a teenager to devote her life to helping people in need. At first, she did this by giving clothes to the poor, visiting the sick, and running a Sunday School in her house where she taught children to read. Then, she received her life's calling when she heard reports from a friend about the conditions in Newgate Prison (see opposite). Visiting the prison for herself in 1813, she found around three hundred women and their children huddled together in two wards and two cells. They were forced to sleep on the floor without any nightclothes or bedding; and some of them were still awaiting their trial (and therefore may well have been innocent).

She visited Newgate on a regular basis, supplying clothing and establishing a school and a chapel there. She also made sure that the women were kept occupied with sewing duties and Bible reading to help in their reformation.

In 1818, she was invited to speak to a House of Commons Committee on London Prisons. She told them how women slept thirty to a room in Newgate, where there were:

> "old and young, hardened offenders with those who had committed only a minor offence or their first crime; the lowest of women with respectable married women and maid-servants".

The committee was impressed with her work, but they disapproved of her views on capital punishment, which she said was "evil and produced evil results". Consequently, little was done.

However, in 1823 the new Home Secretary Sir Robert Peel (most famous for the introduction of the Metropolitan Police Force, also called "Peelers", and later "Bobbies") introduced *The Gaols Act*, which put some of Fry's recommendations into effect; but her work didn't stop there. The Act did not apply to local town gaols (jails) or debtors' prisons (like the one Dickens's father was sent to) and in 1820, Fry published a book which detailed the ongoing problems.

Although she was mostly concerned with prison reform she also campaigned to help the homeless, to improve the conditions in hospitals and mental asylums, and called for reforms to the workhouses. Elizabeth Fry's training school for nurses was a big influence on Florence Nightingale's work, and she even met with Queen Victoria on several occasions. Elizabeth Fry died in 1845.

Newgate Prison

Newgate Prison features heavily in *Great Expectations*; not only because it was the principle prison in London but also because it was regarded as the symbol of crime itself.

The term "Newgate" stems from the days when London was a Roman walled city with eight entrance gates, which also included Ludgate, Bishopsgate and Aldgate – names which have survived in street names to the present day. There had been a prison on the site since the twelfth century. The Great Fire of 1667 destroyed the prison building there at the time, and a new one "of great magnificence" was built in its place. This itself was destroyed by the anti-Catholic "Gordon Rioters" in 1780, when they attacked buildings that represented law and order, and in the process freed around four hundred prisoners. The prison was rebuilt straight away to a new design that incorporated three areas, one for each group of prisoners: debtors, male felons and female felons. Debtors were effectively the only long-term inmates at the prison; the male and female felons were only held there while awaiting trial, execution or transportation to the colonies. As detailed overleaf, prisoners awaiting transportation were mostly held in Prison Hulks that were moored on the River Thames until they received a place on a ship bound for Australia.

The population was increasing, especially in the cities, and this led to extreme poverty; forcing many into a life of crime. In an effort to control the rising crime figures, the government decided to strengthen the law, making many crimes punishable by death (see next page).

As a further deterrent and as a reminder of the law to others, condemned prisoners were hanged in public. Hangings took place at Tyburn, which is near where Marble Arch stands today. "Hanging Days", or "Tyburn Fairs" as they became known, were a renowned, gruesome spectacle. There were eight of them each year, and they were treated as public holidays. Crowds would gather outside Newgate Prison while a bell rang out. Carts would then take the condemned to Saint Sepulchre's Church so that they could be given their "last rites"; and from there they would be taken to Tyburn to be hanged from the gallows. The public would follow them, and become more rowdy and riotous as the journey progressed, rising to a fever pitch when they finally reached the scaffold.

These "Hanging Day" processions themselves posed a threat to law and order; so in 1783 when the Newgate Prison rebuild was completed, it was decided that public hangings would take place in the street outside the prison to avoid having to move the prisoners and incite the public (the Newgate Prison gallows are mentioned in Volume II, Chapter XIII of *Great Expectations*, and appear on page 79 of this book).

Hangings remained public events until 1868, when protests by many, including Dickens, put a halt to these terrible spectacles. Newgate Prison remained in operation until the turn of the century. In 1902, along with the nearby court rooms, it was finally demolished to make way for the Old Bailey. In all, 1120 men and 49 women were hanged there, mostly for burglary, forgery or murder.

The Death Penalty

With the rising crime figures that were a consequence of the abject poverty, the government decided to increase the severity of the law – and particularly the punishment for petty crimes such as theft.

Theft of property under the value of forty shillings (two pre-decimal pounds) carried a seven year prison sentence; theft over that amount was punishable by hanging.

However, not everyone who received the death penalty was executed. Hangings took place in public and were attended by hundreds of people; but before long, the public started to view the condemned as heroic martyrs instead of criminals.

Consequently, the number of hangings had to be reduced.

After receiving the death sentence in the courts, the Court Recorder would prepare his report to the King and Privy Council. In that report, he would indicate which prisoners should hang and which should be granted reprieve. Murderers were hanged within two days of sentencing; but other

criminals had to wait in prison for up to four months to hear their fate. It was quote common for female prisoners to claim that they were pregnant (which they often were!) and force a reprieve that way. Instead of being hanged, prisoners who were granted reprieve were selected for transportation (see below).

Transportation

The idea to ship criminals out of Britain started life nearly two hundred years before Dickens was born (and while Shakespeare was still alive). In 1597, an act was passed to "banish dangerous criminals from the Kingdom"; but it took until 1615 for the first convict ships to leave England. Back then, they were sent to America. This continued for over a hundred and fifty years; but with the War of Independence in 1775, the American colonies closed their ports to British prison ships, and a new destination had to be found. The government decided upon New South Wales (Australia) and the first 778 convicts (586 male, 192 female) left Britain in 1777.

The area formally became a British Colony in 1788, and from then until 1868 when transportation ended, 165,000 convicts were sent there, with only one-in-eight of these being female.

Surprisingly, despite the incredibly long journey of six to twelve months on crowded ships, few prisoners (less than one-in-twenty) died during the voyage. In fact, like Abel Magwitch in this book, many prisoners endured only a short period of confinement or labour, after which they were released "on licence". Although they could not return to Britain, many went on to prosper in their new home.

Prison Hulks

When transportation to America came to an abrupt halt in 1775, and before New South Wales became the replacement destination, a solution had to be found to house the growing number of convicts awaiting deportation. As a temporary solution, they decided to warehouse these convicts in old warships moored in the River Thames. Bought by the prison authorities after the Royal Navy had taken them out of service, these Prison Hulks went on to become long-term fixtures where convicts were held as they waited for the next voyage that would take them away.

Hulks were soon treated as the answer to the generally overcrowded prisons, and were used to detain many prisoners who were not even due to be transported abroad; at one point, over two-thirds of all prisoners were held on hulks. Conditions on these floating prisons were even worse than those on land. One famous hulk, *The Warrior*, comprised three decks, each holding 150 to 200 convicts. The decks were divided into caged cells on both sides of the hull, with a walkway down the middle. Each cell housed eight to ten men, with only the old gun ports in the sides of the hull for ventilation.

Prisoners were forced to sleep with chains around their waists and ankles to prevent them from escaping at night. Any that were found to have made an attempt to file away or otherwise remove them were either flogged, secured with extra irons, or put in solitary confinement.

The hulks were terribly unsanitary. Not only were there problems caused by the overcrowded living conditions, but all water was taken from the polluted Thames; and this gave rise to outbreaks of many diseases, such as cholera, "Gaol Fever" (a form of typhus spread by vermin) and dysentery. Large numbers of prisoners died from these diseases.

By 1850, the use of hulks was in decline; and in 1857, the last hulk was destroyed. Although hulks were no longer in use when Dickens started to write *Great Expectations* (1860), their presence in the book is not an error. The hulks appear at the start of the book, which is set in 1812 — a time when the use of hulks was probably at their peak.

Page Creation

1. Script

The first stage is to adapt the entire story into comic book panels, describing the images to be drawn as well as the dialogue and captions. The challenge that Jen Green faced with *Great Expectations* was how to condense a 400+ page Dickens novel into 140 pages of graphic novel and still retain all the events, details, plot twists and connections. There are two versions of the dialogue and captions: Original Text and Quick Text. Both versions use the same artwork.

Page 19 from the script of *Great Expectations* showing 2 text versions.

2. Character Sheets

Before the script was completed, John Stokes began work on visualising the characters and important scenes. Here you see his sketches of Pip and Miss Havisham. This pre-production is an important stage because it sets the tone for the whole book and enables the artist to develop the final look of the artwork.

3. Rough Sketch

Once the artist receives the script, he takes his character designs and creates rough layouts. John's "roughs" are very detailed. He is considering many things at this stage, including pacing of the action, emphasis of certain elements to tell the story in the best way, lettering space and even lighting of the scene. If any changes need to be made, then it is far easier to make them at this stage, before the page is drawn.

The rough sketch created from the script.

4. Pencils

The process to create the finished artwork begins as soon as the rough sketch is agreed with the editor. The artwork is drawn on A3 art board at approximately 150% of the finished printed size. Because John's roughs are so detailed, very few changes are made when the page is pencilled.

You can see that the tablet has been added in the first panel as a continuity from the previous page, and more lettering space was allowed for in panel 6.

Interestingly, the rough sketch details some artistic elements that won't be tackled until the colouring stage. For example, the last panel shows some night clouds in the rough, but a clear sky in the pencilled page.

The pencil drawing of page 19.

5. Inks

The inking stage is important because it clarifies the pencil lines and finalises the linework. However, inking is not simply tracing over the pencil sketch! It is more like a pre-colouring stage, where black ink is used to fill in shaded areas and to provide texture. A great example of this is in the ironwork on the water pump in panel 5.

The inked image, ready to be coloured.

6. Colouring

Adding colour really brings the page and its characters to life. There is far more to the colouring stage than simply replacing the white areas with flat colour. Some of the linework itself is shaded, while great emphasis is placed upon texture and light sources to get realistic shadows and highlights. Effects are also considered, such as the window glass in panel 1 and the splashing water in panel 5. Finally, the whole page is colour-balanced to the other pages of that scene, and to the overall book.

The final coloured artwork.

7. Lettering

The final stage is to add the captions, sound effects, and speech bubbles from the script. These are laid on top of the finished coloured pages. Two versions of each page are lettered, one for each of the two versions of the book (Original Text and Quick Text).

The finished page 19 with Quick Text lettering.

These lettered images are then saved as final artwork pages and compiled into the finished book.

Below is a comparison showing panel 4 of page 19 in both Original Text and Quick Text versions.

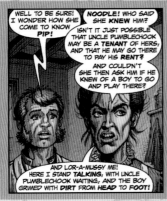

Original Text

THE CLASSIC NOVEL BROUGHT TO LIFE IN FULL COLOUR!

978-1-906332-09-9

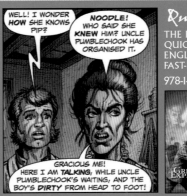

Quick Text

THE FULL STORY IN QUICK MODERN ENGLISH FOR A FAST-PACED READ!

978-1-906332-11-2

Other Classics in the Series

AVAILABLE IN TWO TEXT FORMATS

Each text version uses the same exquisite full-colour artwork providing a completely flexible reading experience — simply choose which version is right for you!

Original Text — THE CLASSIC NOVEL BROUGHT TO LIFE IN FULL COLOUR!

Quick Text — THE FULL STORY IN QUICK MODERN ENGLISH FOR A FAST-PACED READ!

Jane Eyre: The Graphic Novel

• 144 Pages • £9.99
• Script Adaptation: Amy Corzine • Artwork: John M. Burns • Letters: Terry Wiley

This Charlotte Brontë classic is brought to vibrant life by artist John M. Burns. His sympathetic treatment of Jane Eyre's life during the 19th century will delight any reader, with its strong emotions and wonderfully rich atmosphere. Travel back to a time of grand mansions contrasted with the severest poverty, and immerse yourself in this fabulous love story.

Original Text

978-1-906332-06-8

Quick Text

978-1-906332-08-2

Frankenstein: The Graphic Novel

• 144 Pages • £9.99
• Script Adaptation: Jason Cobley • Linework: Declan Shalvey
• Colours: Jason Cardy & Kat Nicholson • Art Direction: Jon Haward • Letters: Terry Wiley

True to the original novel (rather than the square-headed Boris Karloff image from the films!) Declan's naturally gothic artistic style is a perfect match for this epic tale. Frankenstein is such a well known title; yet the films strayed so far beyond the original novel that many people today don't realise how this classic horror tale deals with such timeless subjects as alienation, empathy and understanding beyond appearance.

Original Text

978-1-906332-15-0

Quick Text

978-1-906332-16-7

A Christmas Carol: The Graphic Novel

• 160 Pages • £9.99
• Script Adaptation: Sean Michael Wilson • Pencils: Mike Collins
• Inks: David Roach • Colours: James Offredi • Letters: Terry Wiley

A full-colour graphic novel adaptation of the much-loved Christmas story from the great Charles Dickens. Set in Victorian England and highlighting the social injustice of the time, we see one Ebenezer Scrooge go from oppressor to benefactor when he gets a rude awakening to how his life is, and how it should be. With sumptuous artwork and wonderful characters, this magical tale is a must-have — not only for the festive season, but all year long!

978-1-906332-17-4

978-1-906332-18-1

For more information visit www.classicalcomics.com

Teachers' Resources

To accompany each title in our series of graphic novels, we also publish a set of teachers' resources. These widely acclaimed photocopiable books are designed by teachers, for teachers, to help them meet the requirements of the UK curriculum guidelines. Aimed at ages 10-17, each book provides a broad range of exercises that cover structure, listening, understanding, motivation and comprehension as well as key words, themes and literary techniques. Although the majority of the tasks focus on the use of language in order to align with the framework for teaching English, you will also find many cross-curriculum topics, covering areas within history, ICT, drama, reading, speaking, writing and art; and with a range of skill levels, they provide many opportunities for differentiated teaching and the tailoring of lessons to meet individual needs.

Classical Comics Study Guide: Great Expectations

Black and white, 94 pages, spiral bound A4 (making it easy to photocopy)

Price: £19.99
ISBN: 978-1-906332-13-6

DIFFERENTIATED TEACHING AT YOUR FINGERTIPS!

"Because the exercises feature illustrations from the graphic novel, they provide an immediate link for students between the book and the exercise – however they can also be used in conjunction with any traditional text; and many of the activities can be used completely stand-alone. I think the guide is fantastic and I look forward to using it. I know it will be a great help and lead to engaging lessons. It is easy to use, another major asset. Seriously: well done, well done, well done!"

Dr. Kornel Kossuth,
Head of English, Head of General Studies

"Thank you! These will be fantastic for all our students. It is a brilliant resource and to have the lesson ideas too are great. Thanks again to all your team who have created these."

B.P. KS3

"As to the resource, I can't wait to start using it! Well done on a fantastic service."

Will

"...you've certainly got a corner of East Anglia convinced that this is a fantastic way to teach and progress English literature and language!"

Chris Mehew

"Dear Classical Comics,
Can I just say a quick "thank you" for the excellent teachers' resources that accompanied the *Henry V* Classical Comics. I needed to look no further for ideas to stimulate my class. The children responded with such enthusiasm to the different formats for worksheets, it kept their interest and I was able to find appropriate challenges for all abilities. The book itself was read avidly by even the most reluctant readers. Well done, I'm looking forward to seeing the new titles."

A. Dawes, Tockington Manor School

"The 'Classical Comics' resources that I have used are invaluable for teaching at all levels. My students have found them enormously helpful in preparing for their exams as they have allowed me to create more inventive and imaginative teaching resources."

Dr. Marcella McCarthy,
Leading Teacher for Gifted and Talented Education,
The Cherwell School, Oxford

"Thank you so much. I can't tell you what a help it will be."

A very grateful teacher, Kerryann SA

OUR RANGE OF OTHER CLASSICAL COMICS STUDY GUIDES

Henry V	*Macbeth*	*Jane Eyre*	*Frankenstein*	*A Christmas Carol*
100 pages, Price: £19.99	94 pages, Price: £19.99	96 pages, Price: £19.99	102 pages, Price: £19.99	108 pages, Price: £19.99
ISBN: 978-1-906332-07-5	ISBN: 978-1-906332-10-5	ISBN: 978-1-906332-12-9	ISBN: 978-1-906332-37-2	ISBN: 978-1-906332-38-9

Bringing Classics to Comic Life

Classical Comics has partnered with Comic Life to bring you a unique comic creation experience!

Comic Life is an award-winning software system that is used and loved by millions of children, adults and schools around the world. The software allows you to create astounding comics in a matter of minutes – and it is really easy and fun to use, too!

Through RM Distribution, you can now obtain all of our titles in every text version, electronically for use with any computer or whiteboard system. In addition, you can also obtain our titles as "No Text" versions that feature just the beautiful artwork without any speech bubbles or captions. These files can then be used in Comic Life (or any other

software that can handle jpg files) enabling anyone to create their own version of one of our famous titles.

All of the digital versions of our titles are available from RM on a single user or site-license basis.

For more details, visit www.rm.com and search for Classical Comics, or visit www.classicalcomics.com/education.

Classical Comics, RM and Comic Life - Bringing Classics to Comic Life!